"This Could Get To Be Dangerous, Couldn't It?"

Jake whisp

Martha too   eyes
closed. She   going
to do today   mean,"
she added q

"If you'd open your eyes, I'd tell you."

Reluctantly she complied. Jake was seated on the edge of the bed, a small smile playing about his mouth. "I thought we'd rent a Jeep and take a ride around the island. We could take a picnic lunch. I'd like to look around the hotel on the sly. Maybe we'll see something out of the ordinary."

Martha lifted her chin. "I wonder what your real aim is—to find out about the hotel or to have your way with me."

"Maybe it's a little bit of both."

Martha fixed him with determined blue eyes. "Let's just concentrate on business and leave the enjoyment for some other time," she said sweetly.

"There's no time like the present, sweetheart."

Dear Reader:

Welcome! You hold in your hand a Silhouette Desire – your ticket to a whole new world of reading pleasure.

As you might know, we are continuing the *Man of the Month* concept through to May 1991. In the upcoming year look for special men created by some of our most popular authors: Elizabeth Lowell, Annette Broadrick, Diana Palmer, Nancy Martin and Ann Major. We're sure you will find these intrepid males absolutely irresistible!

But Desire is more than the *Man of the Month*. Each and every book is a wonderful love story in which the emotional and sensual go hand-in-hand. A Silhouette Desire can be humorous or serious, but it will always be satisfying.

For more details please write to:

Jane Nicholls
Silhouette Books
PO Box 236
Thornton Road
Croydon
Surrey
CR9 3RU

KATHERINE GRANGER

TEMPORARY HONEYMOON

Silhouette Desire

Originally Published by Silhouette Books
a division of
Harlequin Enterprises Ltd.

First published in Great Britain in 1990 by Silhouette Books, Eton House, 18-24 Paradise Road, Richmond, Surrey TW9 1SR

© Mary Fanning Sederquest 1990

Silhouette, Silhouette Desire and Colophon are Trade Marks of Harlequin Enterprises B.V.

ISBN 0 373 58012 6

22 – 9011

Made and printed in Great Britain

KATHERINE GRANGER

had never read a romance until 1975, when a friend dumped a grocery bag filled with them in her living room and suggested she might enjoy them. Hooked with the very first one, Ms. Granger became a closet romance writer three years later. When she isn't writing, she teaches creative writing and composition at a community college and freshman composition at her alma mater. Katherine lives in Connecticut with her cat Barnaby. She enjoys movies, theater, golf, the Boston Red Sox, weekends at New England country inns and visits to Cape Cod.

Other Silhouette Books by Katherine Granger

Silhouette Desire

Ruffled Feathers
Unwedded Bliss
He Loves Me, He Loves Me Not
A Match Made in Heaven
Halfway to Heaven

Silhouette Special Edition

No Right or Wrong

One

Jake Molloy stabbed the computer printout with a blunt finger, a scowl darkening his rugged face. "That project on St. Matthew's is way behind schedule. We've got massive work stoppages and cost overruns. Get Bert on the phone, will you, Martha? I want to talk to him."

Martha Simmons nodded and hurried back to her desk. Jake was in the kind of mood she dreaded. Though he seldom got angry, when he did, he became unnaturally quiet, like the calm before a storm. Today he'd been awfully quiet. She was just glad it was Bert Taylor who would be on the receiving end of Jake's tirade. Bert was the construction foreman on the site of the new Hilliard Hotel on St. Matthew's Island in the Caribbean. He was a valued employee, but since being assigned to the job on St. Matthew's, he seemed to have been plagued with bad luck.

She punched in the phone number, then sat back and toyed with her blond hair as she waited for the connection. For the millionth time, she wished her hair was naturally curly and full-bodied, rather than the limp, pale mess that straggled around her shoulders. She had to resort to tying it back with a ribbon to keep herself from looking like a witch.

Sighing, she realized she would never look like a model. At twenty-nine, she had to be content with being smart, practical and efficient. She was a career woman—much to the disappointment of her wealthy parents. They'd wanted a slim, lanky, debutante type with a face that men died for, but they'd ended up with a skinny, awkward daughter who'd excelled only in her studies.

Long ago she'd taken refuge in wearing prim, round-collared blouses, neat A-line skirts, baggy cardigans, and sensible shoes. Eight years after graduating summa cum laude from fashionable Porterville College, she still looked like a coed. She even continued to wear the same horn-rimmed glasses she'd gotten when she was sixteen.

She quickly brought her mind back to business when the phone crackled and popped in her ear, and a weary male voice spoke: "This is Bert."

"Bert, it's Martha in New York. Please hold for Mr. Molloy."

"Ah, jeez, Martha, is he on the rampage again?"

"You know Mr. Molloy, Bert. He likes construction to be on time and under cost. Yours is neither."

"Martha, he's gotta *see* this place! No one would believe it. The natives won't start work unless we sacrifice a damn *chicken* every day!"

Martha smiled. "Is that your cute way of saying St. Matthew's is backward?"

"Hey, I'm not kidding! They really *do* sacrifice chickens. It's some kinda voodoo. They call it boo-koo."

"Boo-koo!" Martha couldn't keep from laughing. "Bert, you better come up with a better excuse than something called boo-koo, or Jake will blow his top."

"Hey, let 'er blow. I can't help it, Martha. I've had it. I'm ready to pack my bags and take the next cargo plane outta here. This place gives me the creeps."

"Hold on, Bert. I'll connect you with Jake."

She put Bert on hold and buzzed her boss. "Jake? Bert's on the line and he doesn't sound happy."

"Who is?" Jake growled, and punched the button that connected him with his foreman.

Martha silently wished Bert well in his battle with the boss, then began typing a letter on her computer. A few minutes later, Jake's bellow shook the office doors.

"Martha? Get in here!"

Martha sighed, stood and snatched her steno pad and pen, then went sailing into Jake's office. She was the only one on the staff who wasn't afraid of him. In her employment interview five years earlier she'd somehow sensed that Jake's bark was worse than his bite, and she hadn't let him rattle her. Impressed by her cool, unflappable demeanor, he'd hired her on the spot, turning away a bevy of prettier but far less capable secretarial candidates.

"Are we angry, Mr. Molloy?" she asked brightly, taking a seat opposite his wide cherrywood desk.

Jake eyed her balefully. He didn't know why he put up with her smart-alecky manner, except by now he was used to it. And he supposed he even sort of liked it. Martha didn't cower in front of him as most people did, and he respected that. She was a plain Jane, but she was more than a secretary. She knew the hotel business inside out and was his right hand. He didn't know what he would do without her sound judgement and practical advice. Sink, he supposed, chuckling to himself; he certainly wouldn't swim.

He put an elbow on his desk and rested his squared chin in his palm. "We've got problems on St. Matthew's."

"So I hear. Something about chickens."

Jake shook his head and leaned back, stretching to rid the kinks from his neck. He yanked at his tie and unbuttoned the top button of his white shirt. As he talked, he rolled up his sleeves. "It stinks, Martha. Something's not right. Bert swears it's all the natives' fault. He says they're holding up work because of this magic of theirs called boo-koo."

Martha raised a calm brow. "Sounds like you're not buying that."

Jake rubbed his chin, narrowing his gray eyes thoughtfully. "Nope, I'm not. I've built hotels in Africa and on every Caribbean island there is. So St. Matthew's is the most undeveloped. So what? Hell, I'd sacrifice Colonel Sanders himself if it would get construction moving, but it's gotta be more than that, Martha. Maybe some smart little native is flying out the construction equipment to the black market as fast as we fly it in. Or maybe Bert's taking a little payola from the competition."

"Jake, you are the least trusting man I've ever met. You hired and trained Bert yourself. As for the others on the site, Bert hired them. Can't you let Bert solve the problem?"

"If Bert could have dealt with this on his own, he would have already. The problem is, he can't. He admitted himself that he's stymied. I have to go down there and snoop around. Something's rotten in St. Matthew's, so to speak. The only thing is, I just can't waltz in and announce I'm investigating skulduggery."

"Why not?"

"Because on a small island like St Matthew's, the problem could be anyone. There are three hotels on the island, all locally owned. Any one of them could resent an international biggie like Hilliard Hotels building there. For half a century, they've had the island to themselves. Now we're horning in, and they might not like it. Progress can be threatening to some folks. Uh-uh, Martha. I need to have a good excuse for visiting the island—one that's not even remotely connected with Hilliard Hotels."

"You could go on vacation," Martha suggested.

"You know how strange it looks for a man to go on vacation by himself?"

Martha shrugged. "Take a girlfriend."

Jake glared. "Don't have one."

"Get one."

Jake ignored her comment and laced his fingers behind his head. "Now why on earth would a man go to a Caribbean island?" he mused.

"After a vacation, the only reason I can think of is a honeymoon," Martha said offhandedly. Personally, she thought Jake was overreacting. If he wasn't such a stickler for efficiency and speed, he wouldn't even have a problem. Who cared if the construction project was a few months behind schedule?

"That's it," Jake announced, breaking into her reverie.

"What's it?"

"A honeymoon."

She stared at him blankly. "You lost me."

"I'll go there on my honeymoon," Jake explained.

"But you just admitted you don't even have a girlfriend."

"That's right, but I have a faithful secretary."

She stared at him, then began to laugh. "You're crazy. You can't mean what I think you mean."

"It would work, Martha. We'd get married by a justice of the peace and fly down to St. Matthew's for a two- or three-week honeymoon."

"Jake, you can't be serious."

"Why not? I trust you—you're about the only person on earth I *do* trust—and you know the business inside and out, so you'd be a help rather than a hindrance." He eyed her critically. "Of course, we'd have to fix you up a bit."

"Fix me—" She broke off, offended to the core. "What's the matter? I'm not good enough the way I am?"

"Sweetheart, you're the best secretary on earth, and I'd never dream of trying to change you in the office. It's in the bedroom I'm worried about."

"The—" Her face turned bright red as she tried to get her voice to work. She felt as if she were strangling on fifteen dozen words that were all trying to get out at once. "Listen, Mr. Molloy—"

"Now stop being apoplectic and just sit back and listen for a minute," Jake said. "First off, I want you with me. What other way could we manage that? If I brought you there without marrying you, it would look like you and I were enjoying a bit on the side, wouldn't it? And what would that do for your reputation?"

"It would just about destroy it," Martha retorted. "Now, will you stop this foolishness and get serious?"

"I am serious. I have no intention of ruining your reputation, Martha. When our little investigation is over, we'll come back to New York, quietly get the marriage annulled and that will be that."

"And what about the rest of the staff? What will they say? Everyone will be staring at us, wondering what happened, talking about us behind our backs. It won't work, Jake. I refuse to go along with your little ruse."

"Who cares what people say?" Jake asked. "Anyway, it will work, and you will go along with it because you're the best secretary in the world and you love this job as much as I do. You and I are married to Hilliard Hotels International, Martha, and you know it as well as I do. Now stop protesting and let's start planning our attack."

"My God, you're really serious," she observed wonderingly.

"I sure am," Jake replied, sitting forward enthusiastically. "First, you'll have to make reservations at one of the hotels. See if you can get a honeymoon suite. Tell them you and your boyfriend decided to get married on the spur of the moment. Then schedule us for blood tests and find a justice of the peace." He paused and looked at her, gesturing in-articulately with a large hand. "And then do something about your hair. Go to a department store and get a make-up job or something. Get contact lenses instead of those awful horn-rimmed spectacles. Buy some frilly clothes."

"Frilly clothes?" she repeated, turning up her nose, along with the tone of her voice.

"You know, the kind of thing a woman wears on her honeymoon. Sexy stuff. Lacy negligees and black strapless dresses."

"On a secretary's budget?" she asked incredulously.

"No, sweetheart, on the company's budget. It's all part of the investigation."

"And who's going to okay it? The president himself?"

"Martha, when Jim Hilliard promoted me to vice president in charge of new hotel development, he gave me carte blanche. I'm the boss here. I don't need anyone to okay how I spend my money."

Martha stared at Jake, then grumbled under her breath. "I'm going to look ridiculous."

"What'd you say?"

"I said I'm going to look ridiculous!" she repeated loudly. "Honestly, Jake, I'm not the kind of woman who looks good in black strapless dresses. I'm tall and gangly and I trip over my own feet. I'll go along with marrying you for a few weeks, but this makeover stuff won't work."

"Sure, it will. I had a cousin who had a complete make-over. I think they analyzed her colors, or something crazy like that. Then they taught her to apply makeup and re-styled her hair—I didn't even recognize her when I saw her. Believe me, if it worked for Hilda, it'll work for you."

"Hilda was that bad, eh?" Martha commented sardoni-cally.

"Hilda was a mess," Jake exclaimed, then looked stricken. "Not that you're a mess! Not at all! You just need a little . . . er . . . polishing."

"Oh? What am I? Silver?"

"And that's another thing, Martha—you'll have to change your tone on St. Matthew's. A sharp tongue's fine in a secretary, but no man in his right mind would marry a woman who lets him have it the way you do."

"Wait just a darn minute," Martha returned tightly. "Is this an investigation about work delays on St. Matthew's or a complete makeover for Martha Simmons? Next you'll be suggesting plastic surgery."

"Only if it would shut you up for a few weeks."

She lifted her chin but couldn't stop the two patches of red from forming in her cheeks. "I wasn't aware that I annoyed you so much, Mr. Molloy," she said primly. "Perhaps you should choose a more suitable companion to accompany you to St. Matthew's."

"Cut the lip, Martha," Jake replied, rubbing his eyes tiredly. "I have more problems on St. Matthew's than I can shake a stick at, and now you're getting in on the game."

"Only because you asked me to," she pointed out. "It wasn't my idea to marry you and go on a foolish honeymoon to some godforsaken island where they worship chickens."

"They don't worship them, Martha," he explained. "They kill them."

"Even worse."

Jake sighed and began sorting through files on his desk. "Go shopping, Martha. Buy up a storm. Have a facial and a hair thingamajig. Get your nails done. Order those contacts. But first of all, make the reservations on St. Matthew's. I don't want any screwups. When we get there, I want everything to go smooth as strawberries and cream."

Martha remained seated. "Mr. Molloy, there's something we haven't discussed."

"Oh, right. The money. Make out a check for five thousand and I'll sign it. That should cover your expenses, shouldn't it?"

"It's not money I'm worried about, Mr. Molloy."

He looked up from a file he'd been studying. "Oh? What is it, then? Don't worry about vacation time—this won't affect it. You'll still get your usual three weeks off."

"It's not vacation time, either, I'm afraid."

Jake closed the file and met Martha's gaze. "All right then, what haven't I thought about, Miss Efficiency?"

Martha shifted uncomfortably in her chair. "You're really serious about our getting married, is that right?"

"Right as rain."

"Then I think we need to discuss this arrangement in more detail."

"What's to discuss? We'll have the blood tests, find a justice of the peace, hop a plane for Puerto Rico, then change to a commuter plane to St. Matthew's. We'll stay at one of the hotels on the island. I'll sniff around—you'll sniff around. We find out what's causing the work delays and cost overruns on the new project, settle the matter, come home, have the marriage annulled and go on happily ever after. It's simple, Martha."

"Except for the small matter of sleeping together."

Her quiet words were as explosive as gunpowder in a flaming building. Jake stared at her, then dropped his head in his hands and kneaded his temples. "You mean that's a problem?"

Astounded, Martha sat up straight, her back as rigid as a poker. "You mean it isn't?"

"Oh, jeez," he said. "I think we have a little communication problem here."

"That's funny," Martha commented, "I didn't think we had any at all."

"All right, all right, I get your drift. So we haven't talked about that. I just assumed—"

"Assumed what, Mr. Molloy? That we would sleep together? Or we wouldn't?"

"Well, we'll have to sleep together, Martha. We're going to be married, after all."

She opened her eyes wide in pretended ignorance. "You mean I can't ask for twin beds in the honeymoon suite?"

He leaned forward, his face dark with irritation. "Ask for the biggest, widest, softest bed on the premises. But don't for a minute think it's because I have any plans for either it or you, Ms. Simmons. This is a business arrangement and it will remain a business arrangement. Does that calm your worries? Your virtue will remain intact, I assure you."

"I didn't mean to make a big deal out of it, Mr. Molloy," she sniffed. "It was just something I felt we should discuss."

"And quite rightly, too." He sighed and slumped back in his chair, putting a foot up on his desk and swiveling back and forth. "Look. We'll have to pretend we're in love, Martha, or it won't work. When we're in public, we'll probably have to act a little lovey-dovey or people might get suspicious. But I swear to you, once we're in the privacy of our room, things will be as impersonal and businesslike between us as they have been the past five years."

"Even when I'm in my see-through black negligee?" she asked ironically.

For a moment he looked as if he couldn't picture Martha in anything but narrow skirts and high-necked blouses. Then he seemed to shake himself and find a response to her question. "Martha, I'm a grown man. I'm long past the fever of youth when the sight of a woman sets my blood on fire. I can control myself, as I'm sure you can control yourself. We're both adults—let's credit ourselves with that, at least."

"Then why do I have to buy frilly nighties at all?" she demanded. "I'll feel ridiculous, parading around in front of you, half dressed."

"Look, I'm sure you'll feel a little awkward at first, just as I might, but we have to put up a good front, Martha.

There'll be maids snooping around, any one of whom might be on the payroll of someone who's trying to get Hilliard Hotels to give up on its new project on St. Matthew's.''

"Are you trying to tell me that a housemaid might be a *spy*?''

"I know that sounds melodramatic to you, but it's true. The first rule of business is, never trust anyone. If we're going down there to investigate, we have to look as believable as possible. If we're holding hands over dinner, but then you run around in flannel nightgowns and sleep on the couch, the maids will start talking. And who knows who might overhear them. Uh-uh, Martha. We have to do this right, or we can't do it at all.''

Martha mulled over his words. "I suppose I see what you're getting at, but it still won't be easy for me.''

"Look at it as part of your job," he suggested. "Pretend we're industrial spies. Hilliard Hotel's future on St. Matthew's depends on us. We've already sunk over five million dollars on that island. We're going down there to assure that our investment comes to fruition. Nothing more.''

"Well, when you put it that way—''

"That's the only way you *can* put it," Jake said, relaxing for the first time in five minutes. "It's a job, and someone's gotta do it. We're the ones, Martha. It all comes down to company loyalty.''

"Company loyalty," Martha repeated. "Why, yes. That is what it's all about, isn't it?''

Jake rubbed his mouth to keep from revealing a grin. "You bet, Martha.''

"Well!" she responded brightly, rising to leave his office. "I'll get on those reservations. The blood tests should be a simple matter of finding a nearby lab and taking the time to get blood drawn. I'm sure a justice of the peace will be able to fit us in in the next week or so. We'll need witnesses, of course.''

"In the movies they just drag people in off the street."

"Won't that look funny?"

"To whom?"

"Well, I was thinking of everyone we work with. Maybe it would seem more of a love match if we asked someone here to stand up for us."

"Yeah, I can see your point. I suppose you'll want to invite your parents also."

"Ha!" Martha retorted sardonically. "Not on your life. My parents have never approved of anything I've ever done, much less of the men I've brought home to meet them. I gave up trying to please them ages ago. No, it would be better for all concerned if they never even find out about this little month-long mission. Why don't you ask your assistant, Dave Schneider, and I'll ask Laurie Anderson. Neither of them gossip, but they'll be sure to let it slip when we return that we really were married."

"Okay, I think you're right. I'll talk to Dave and you speak with Laurie. Just be sure to impress on Laurie that you don't want it getting around until we come back from the honeymoon. All we need is someone showing up on the island who knows us. And Martha?"

She turned at the door. "Yes?"

"Take the rest of the afternoon off. Start on that shopping spree. Don't come back till you've bought out the store."

She tilted her head and considered him. Seated in a plush office suite in New York, he seemed an anomaly. He looked as if he truly belonged on a construction site, wearing chambray shirts, faded jeans and leather workboots. He was tall and solidly built, with a rugged face and a jaw that seemed to have been chipped from granite. Everything about him communicated power, from the muscular bulk of his torso to the confident way he made decisions.

"The shopping spree can wait," she replied. "I think I'd better make those reservations. If we can't get a room on St. Matthew's, the whole scheme will blow up in our faces before we even get a chance to put it in action."

"Right, as usual. See why I need to take you with me? You organize me, Martha. You're the practical one."

"And what are you, Mr. Molloy?"

He waved a large hand. "Damned if I know. I just dream up these schemes. You're the one I need to put them into action."

Martha smiled as she slipped out of the office. Despite her initial misgivings, she was excited. She hadn't done anything as outlandish as this since she was seventeen years old and ran away with Greg Miller. Her parents had had a fit. They'd called the state police, wrung their hands in apprehension, then watched openmouthed as a tired, bedraggled Greg Miller had returned their daughter at half past two in the morning.

"She's too much for me," he'd lamented, falling into a chair and begging for a glass of cola. "I thought I loved her," he'd complained, head in his hands. "I thought we'd be happy together."

"And you weren't?" Mr. Simmons had asked, rocking back on his heels as he scowled at his defiant daughter.

"Gee, no!" Greg had exclaimed. "Martha's the bossiest girl I ever met! I couldn't even make a right-hand turn without her telling me to turn left."

"Well, it's a good thing you discovered this before it was too late," Mrs. Simmons had said haughtily.

"Yeah," Greg had admitted with a sigh, scratching his belly. "Think I'll go home now. My parents will be worried sick."

Martha had sat on the sofa watching her hero slowly sink before her very eyes. From that day on, men had never been quite the same.

Perhaps, she thought, settling down at her desk, things were going to start changing....

Two

Laurie Anderson stared at Martha with wide brown eyes. "You're *what*?" she cried.

"I'm marrying Jake," Martha said under her breath, looking around the restaurant uneasily. "And don't be so loud, Laurie. I don't want anyone else to find out."

"Why not? It's fabulous!" Laurie looked Martha up and down and seemed to come to the conclusion that miracles really did happen. "Ya-zoo Christmas!" she exclaimed soulfully. "You're marrying Jake Molloy. I can't believe your luck."

Martha sat up a little straighter, unable to hide the small hint of irritation that tugged at her. Why did Laurie think it was just a matter of luck? So what if she wasn't the most beautiful woman on earth? Did it seem so impossible that a man like Jake would ever find her attractive?

"Hey, I'm sorry," Laurie apologized, reaching out to lightly touch Martha's wrist. "I'm really happy for you, Martha. It's just that it's such a surprise. I mean, who'd think you and Jake Molloy—" She broke off. "Oh, brother, I did it again. I'm sorry, Martha. It's just that you never acted like anything was going on between you two and *he* never acted like it and..." Laurie's words drifted off. She shrugged lamely. "Hey, I'd love to stand up for you. I can't tell you how happy I am for you."

"You just can't believe Jake Molloy would ever find me attractive, that's what you're really thinking, isn't it?" Martha asked quietly.

"Well, I have to admit, at first it really threw me. But now that I'm getting used to the idea, I think it's terrific. I didn't know he had enough brains to recognize gold when he saw it."

Martha stared at her friend wonderingly. "You mean it?"

"Sure, I mean it!" Laurie said staunchly. "You're one in a million, Martha. You're like the difference between fool's gold and the real thing."

Martha smiled but lowered her gaze to her hands. It was nice to hear that a friend believed in her, but Martha knew too well that what Laurie thought had happened hadn't happened at all. Jake hadn't seen beneath the colorless façade to the real woman who lurked beneath, because there *wasn't* a real woman underneath. There was just Martha, pale and tall and awkward. With Martha, what you saw was what you got.

Martha sighed and forced a bright smile. "Well, anyway, we're getting married Friday morning and hopping a plane for Puerto Rico."

"But you hate to fly!" Laurie exclaimed. "When I asked you to go to Club Med with me, you refused because we'd have to go by plane."

"Well, I'm older now," Martha explained lamely. "I'll be a married woman. I can't let a childish fear get to me."

"Oh, Martha," Laurie said affectionately. "It sounds like Jake's doing wonders for you. I hope you two will really be happy."

Martha quickly ducked her head and pretended to search for something in her pocketbook. She would feel like a hypocrite and a liar if she acknowledged Laurie's wish. Only she and Jake knew just how long they would live together, and it sure wouldn't be "happily ever after."

Martha looked up hesitantly at her more attractive friend. Laurie might be five years her junior, but in experience she was decades older. She had a flair for clothes, and she turned men's heads wherever she went. "Look, Laurie, Jake wants me to buy some clothes and I'd like your help. You've got great taste. Would you be able to come shopping with me?"

"Would I?" whooped Laurie. "You just stand back, kiddo! We'll blaze a swath through the designer boutiques that'll look like Sherman taking Atlanta. Charge! That's my motto! Let's see, you'll need about a dozen sexy little nighties and some lacy bras and bikini panties—"

"You really think I can pull that stuff off?" Martha asked. "I mean, I'll feel a little stupid buying all that sexy stuff."

"Well, honey, Jake obviously enjoys your company enough to want it every night for the rest of his life. Why not treat him to a Martha he doesn't know exists?" Laurie laughed at the look of embarrassment on her friend's face. "Just leave it to me. We'll have you looking like a sex bombette."

"Good grief, I'll look ridiculous," Martha protested. "I'm not the type, Laurie."

"Well, Jake Molloy obviously thinks you are, so we're not going to disappoint him."

Martha gulped back the urge to sob. More than anything, she wished she could confide in her friend, but she couldn't. After all this was over, when she and Jake had completed their business on St. Matthew's and were back in Manhattan, marriage effectively annulled, she would sit Laurie down and tell her all about it.

* * *

Martha stood in the bridal department, bewitched by the dozens of gowns that graced the mannequins. A haze of snowy white wedding dresses surrounded her, with gossamer veils, floating trains, bodices and sleeves adorned with pearls and iridescent sequins in swirling patterns of butterflies and flowers.

"Are you *sure* you can't wear a bridal gown?" Laurie wailed. "Look at this one! It'd be gorgeous on you! Or *this* one..." Laurie held up a gown and moaned in ecstasy, her curly blond hair drifting like a cloud around her pretty face. "Oh, Martha, someday I want a dress just like this. I'd die for this dress."

Transfixed, Martha simply stared. Laurie would indeed be a beautiful bride someday, but right now they had more urgent things to do. Mentally squaring her shoulders, Martha tugged at her friend's arm.

"Come on, Laurie, these gowns are beautiful but they're not for me. I thought a simple little beige suit would be nice."

"A suit!" Laurie shrieked, wrinkling her nose in displeasure. "No way! If you won't buy one of these confections, then you'll at least find a lovely dress. Maybe something in white with sequins on the shoulders. Something simple but stunning. And we'll fix your hair and see about getting you contact lenses—I always said you needed contacts, Martha—and a makeup session with Miss Doreen. She's the best. Costs an arm and a leg, but who cares, you're marrying Jake Molloy, right?"

"Well, Jake isn't exactly made out of money."

"Course he is! He's dripping in the stuff. All big execs are. It's part of their job description." Laurie pulled Martha close and muttered in her ear. "You listen to me, sweetie—establish the lines of combat right now. Demand a big budget for clothes. Insist on it, or once you're married awhile and the glow wears off, he'll pull in the checkbook and put it under lock and key. They all do. Men are built with little spending-detectors buried just under their skin."

"You make them sound like little guys from outer space."

"Most of them are," Laurie replied, rolling her eyes. "I *hope* Jake's different. But just to be safe, buy lots of stuff now so he gets used to it. Break him in real good, Martha, or you'll spend the rest of your life begging for a five spot to have tea with the girls."

Martha laughed off Laurie's comments, but as they headed to the designer dress department, her gaze traveled from side to side like radar, taking in the glories of the dresses that graced the racks. She felt like a princess, surrounded by dozens and dozens of wondrous things, each more beautiful, more exciting than the last.

"Oh, Laurie," she breathed, spying a prefect dress. "Look at it."

"Which one? That ugly pink?"

"No, silly, the white one. Just like you said—simple but stunning." Martha ran her hand over the creamy wool, swimming in visions of herself wearing the dress. But it wasn't the real Martha she saw; it was a radiant Martha, a beautiful woman with a smashing figure and bouncing gold hair like Laurie's.

"It's perfect for you!" Laurie squealed.

"Oh, come on," Martha said, holding the dress up and fighting the urge to drool over it. "I'd never be able to carry it off. I'm not the type to wear something like this."

"Why? 'Cause it's not some cruddy little businesslike beige suit? Of *course* you can wear it. It'd be perfect on you. You're so classy, Martha. All you need to do is change your hair and wear a little makeup."

"Classy? Me?"

"Sure. Look at your bones. My mom always told me that the most beautiful women in the world have good bone structure. Your bones are top-notch. You're lean like a thoroughbred, Martha. You just gotta flaunt it for a change, instead of hiding it under a baggy old cardigan and shapeless skirt."

Martha shook her head and put the dress back on the rack. "No way. I'll find a simple little suit, and that's final. This just isn't me."

"Martha," Laurie insisted, tearing the dress off the rack, "stop being such an old priss and put this dress on now!"

"I'll look silly. It's not me."

"Martha," Laurie threatened.

"But it's not, I tell you!"

"Martha." Laurie put her hand on her hip and jutted out her lower lip. "You want me to fling myself on the floor and start screaming?"

"Oh, all right." Martha sighed. "But you just wait. You'll see. I can't wear sophisticated stuff like this...."

"Oh, Martha," Laurie exclaimed when Martha emerged from the dressing room moments later. "It's you. Turn around." Laurie nodded, her face glowing. "Oh, yes. It's perfect. It's exactly right."

Even Martha couldn't disagree. She'd never worn such a beautiful dress in her life, and she couldn't get over the difference it made. She looked like another woman. Not that she was suddenly beautiful, or striking, or even pretty; but there was something about the dress that changed her. She supposed it was because it made her look less businesslike and more like a woman.

"Oh, Laurie," she gasped, "it is beautiful, isn't it?"

"Wonderful," her friend agreed. "And with spike heels and your hair swept up on your head and pearl or diamond earrings, you'll be a knockout."

"Spike heels?" Martha laughed. "I've never worn spike heels in my life! I'd trip over myself and break a leg."

"Will you give yourself credit for once?" Laurie demanded. "Come on, Martha, stop saying no before you've even tried something."

"Well, Jake *did* tell me to buy some clothes...."

"Of course he did! And you're going to. By the time we're finished, you'll be the best-dressed bride on Puerto Rico."

"Oh, we're not—" Martha stopped herself before she gave away their honeymoon destination.

"You're not what?" Laurie demanded, a knowing twinkle in her eyes. "You're not going to be dressed too much of the time?"

"Laurie!"

"Oh, come on," Laurie teased, inching toward Martha. "What's he like?"

"What's who like?"

"Come *on*, Martha, what's *Jake* like?"

"What do you mean, what's he like? You know him. He's just Jake."

"Stop playing coy, will you? What's he like in bed? I'll bet he's *gorgeous*! I swear that man got muscles before God handed out anything to any other man on earth."

Martha stared at Laurie as if seeing her for the first time. This was an entire side to friendship she'd never experienced. In boarding school and later in college, she'd always heard the other girls giggling and swapping stories about their boyfriends, but since Martha had had so few dates, she'd never really been included.

Martha turned back to the image of perfection in the mirror. It was all just pretense, she thought, but she was going to enjoy it while she could. Later, when she came home from St. Matthew's, she would face the music. Right now, she was going to have a ball.

"Hey," Laurie said softly. "Did I offend you talking that way about you and Jake? I'm sorry, Martha. I didn't mean to pry. Sometimes I think me and my big mouth should be kicked into the next country. Like Canada, maybe. Or across the ocean to France."

Reaching out, Martha put her arms around her friend. "Hush," she told her, laughing. "You've been terrific

Laurie. I won't have you saying mean things about your-self.''

"Oh, Martha, I'm so happy for you." Laurie hugged Martha hard. "I wish you tons of joy and happiness un-ending.''

Tears welled up in Martha's eyes but she held them back, squeezed them in behind closed lids while holding on to Laurie for dear life, filled with the strangest mixture of joy and pain she'd ever known. Suddenly it struck her that she was really and truly getting married. It might be for only a short time, but she was finally getting to experience all the wonderful things most women took for granted. But she, herself, never had. She'd graduated from college with the expectation of never marrying. She'd been excited about having a career. Now she saw how she'd circumscribed her life within the narrow confines of being just a career woman.

Turning back to the mirror, she looked at herself with new eyes—eyes that suddenly saw new possibilities; possibilities that until today had never even seemed real.

"You got your blood test, right?" Martha asked.

Jake nodded, his head buried in a report on the lack of progress on St. Matthew's.

"And you got the marriage license?" Martha asked, bit-ing on the end of her pen while scanning her checklist.

"Yup."

"Well, I'm glad to see you're so excited about the wed-ding tomorrow."

"Um," he grunted, and continued reading.

"I bought some clothes," she finally ventured.

"Uh-huh."

She stared at the man who would be her husband by this time tomorrow. "I'll be wearing a tobacco sack dyed bright red."

"Oh?"

"Yes," she said airily. "And black galoshes and a pink velvet fedora, and I'll be carrying a sack of pigs."

Jake peered at her from over the top of his report. "You trying to scare me out of this thing?"

She smiled wryly. "No, just trying to get your attention."

"You succeeded." He put down the report. "So what's on your mind?"

She sat down facing him. Since he'd hatched his crazy scheme a week ago they'd barely discussed it. "Jake, I want to make sure you really want to go through with this."

"Well, of course I do. What makes you even ask?"

"You've barely mentioned it, for one thing."

"Sweetheart, I'm up to my behind in problems. I don't have time to contemplate a wedding."

"Even if it's your own?"

He considered her awhile, then said, "Maybe you're the one who's having second thoughts."

She squirmed in her chair and fidgeted with her pen. "Why would you say a silly thing like that?"

He threw his report down and got up and walked around to the front of his desk. Leaning against it, he folded his muscular arms and stared at her. "Okay, Miss Martha, out with it. What's bothering you?"

"Nothing. Absolutely nothing."

He sighed and pulled up a chair, running a distracted hand through his hair. "Last time I heard that, I had to fire the guy."

"There's still time to fire me."

He nodded. "Last-minute jitters, eh?"

She shrugged and smiled a little. "I guess so. It's just that it's suddenly real and I guess I'm a little worried."

"About what? Posing as a bride? You'll do great—tobacco sack, galoshes, pigs and all."

"So you *were* listening!"

"Both ears."

She looked down at her hands, locked together in her lap as if in mortal combat. Lately she'd been wringing her hands a lot. It wasn't a habit she was used to.

"I guess it's more than worry, Jake. It's—" She frowned, trying to catch the exact nuance that had been escaping her these past few days. "It's almost like superstition—"

"Superstition?" he interrupted. "So what do you want to do? Sacrifice a sacred chicken at the ceremony tomorrow?"

"Jake."

"Okay, I'm sorry. Go on with what you were saying. I just thought a joke might make you feel better."

She nodded, but felt a vast sense of aloneness. She was trying to explain what was in her heart, and Jake made a joke. It was the last thing she needed, but she realized they didn't really know each other, despite having worked together for five years. Yet tomorrow morning they would be husband and wife. Granted, for only a few short weeks, but that was precisely what seemed wrong.

"Jake," she finally said, "I've always believed that marriage is sacred, but what we're doing tomorrow...it's as if we're cheating somehow, not playing by the rules. I don't know, I suppose it sounds crazy, but I feel as if we're doing something we shouldn't be doing."

"Because we're pretending?"

She hesitated. "Yes, I suppose that's part of it."

"What's the other part?"

She stared down at her hands, still knotted in her lap. She could see the image of her wedding dress imprinted in her mind's eye. Every night she'd tried it on, staring at herself in the mirror. And every night the feeling had grown stronger and stronger, a feeling intense but so far unnameable, filling her with a deep sense of loneliness and loss.

"Jake," she continued, lifting her gaze to his, her eyes filled with pain, "I can't help it, but I'm feeling what a woman feels when she gets married. The problem is, I know it's just a sham, that it'll end almost before it starts. And somehow that makes me feel cheated—as if this is the only chance I'll ever get, and it's being ruined."

She dipped her head and stared miserably at her hands. Why had she even brought it up? He wouldn't understand. No man could. Marriage was special to a woman. To a man, it meant added responsibility, perhaps, but it didn't fulfill him—not the way it did so many women. To Jake this marriage was just a business arrangement—something he needed to accomplish a goal.

She stole a look at Jake and to her surprise saw that he looked troubled, as if her words had touched something in him she hadn't suspected was there. "Jake, I'm sorry," she said hurriedly. "I shouldn't have said anything."

"No," he disagreed. "I'm glad you did." He frowned and rubbed his jaw. "I'm just not real good at this kind of thing, I guess."

"What kind of thing?" she asked softly, feeling almost sorry for him. He looked so uncomfortable, so ill at ease, that she wanted to comfort him, to tell him he shouldn't worry over her silly problems.

"I'm not good at talking about women's feelings." He sighed and thrust his legs out, burying his hands in his trouser pockets as he scowled at the floor. "Matter of fact, I'm not good at talking about feelings at all—anyone's. But—" He looked up and met her gaze. "it sounds as if you feel like I'm using you."

She hesitated, then realized she couldn't answer. She did feel she was being used; and at the bottom of that recognition lay anger. Yet she'd agreed with his plan, so she didn't have a right to feel angry. Miserable, she dropped her gaze to her hands, unable to articulate her feelings.

Jake sighed and began to pace. "In a way, I guess I am using you," he finally admitted. "I never thought about how this might upset your life. Come to think of it, I never thought of you at all. I just took it for granted you'd do it. I just wish you'd have backed out sooner."

"I'm not backing out, Jake," she replied softly.

"You aren't?"

She shook her head. "I'm just expressing what I feel, or trying to. Actually, I'm so mixed up, I'm not exactly sure *what* I feel."

"Well, that makes two of us," he growled.

"What exactly do you mean by that?" she sniffed.

"Aw, jeez, Martha, why do you women always have to go and analyze everything? We have a nice thing going. All the arrangements are made and there aren't any complications. Let's just keep it that way, okay?"

"That is so typical of a man!" Martha cried. "You ask a woman to marry you—"

"Now wait just a darned minute. I never asked you to marry me. I suggested that we marry each other to solve a problem on St. Matthew's. It's a business deal, honey, not an affair of the heart."

"Fine," she answered stiffly, rising from her chair. "I wouldn't have it any other way."

"You think I would?" he crowed. "Hell, the day I marry a woman will be the day they bury me at sea."

"Then get ready for a wet funeral tomorrow, buddy," she retorted, and stalked out the door.

Jake stared after her, then shook his head. Women. They were the only mistake God had ever made, but they were sure a doozy.

Three

———

Martha consulted her checklist, pen in hand. Yesterday's last-minute jitters and doubts were behind her. She was herself again, efficient and practical, supervising the loading of her suitcases into the taxi that would take her to the justice of the peace.

Feeling strangely naked, she had packed her horn-rimmed spectacles and was wearing her new contact lenses. The fake diamond earrings Laurie had pressed on her were replaced with simple but elegant gold hoops, but she couldn't find anything wrong with the way Laurie had done her hair. Earlier that morning she had swept it into a sophisticated French twist, and Martha found herself staring at her image, unable to believe the changes in her appearance. The makeover artist at the cosmetics counter had outdone herself! Martha still couldn't believe how tweezed eyebrows, a little blusher and eye make up could make her look so different. She wondered what Jake would say when he saw her.

She snorted to herself. Probably nothing. Knowing Jake, he probably wouldn't even see her. He would be too busy juggling spy schemes in his head to notice the woman he was about to marry.

"Don't forget that small one," Martha said to the cab-driver, who had already struggled up and down four flights of stairs with three of her five suitcases. "That's the one with the crown jewels in it," she added dryly.

The driver glanced at her. "You goin' someplace far away, lady?"

"Mmm," she replied. "Might as well be Timbuktu."

"Yeah? Where's that?"

She dismissed his question with a wave of her hand and returned to studying her list. Plane tickets, proof of citizenship, hotel reservations—all were in order. She'd lowered the heat, left her plants with a neighbor and stopped the newspaper delivery.

"All right," she announced. "This is it. Let's get going."

"We off to the airport?" the driver asked as they trudged down the stairs.

"No, we're going someplace on Fifth Avenue." She searched in her pocketbook for the address of the justice of the peace. "Yes, here it is," she said, giving the driver the address.

"You mean I gotta unload all these suitcases there?"

"No, you simply have to park and wait for me. Don't worry about the fare—I'll pay it. I'm getting married. It should only take a few minutes. Then we'll go to the airport from there. My...er...fiancé has already sent his luggage to the airport."

The driver stopped descending the stairs and turned to stare at her. "You gettin' married? Whatsamatta? No flowers? No reception? Not even a glass of champagne?"

"I'm afraid not. Haven't you heard? Romance is out."

"Hey, lady, say it ain't so! Me and the wife, we still sit and hold hands when we watch television. Eat a little popcorn, snuggle, sneak a kiss during the commercials. Hey, that's the life."

Martha peered at the driver, interested despite herself. "Really? How long have you been married?"

"Three years awready." He nodded, grinning. "I'm savin' for my own cab. Gonna have my own business someday. Loretta, she works in the cafeteria at a school. We're doin' real well."

"Do you...do you have children yet?" Martha asked softly.

The driver broke into a grin. "Yeah. One little guy. Named after me. Danny, Junior."

Martha's eyes unexpectedly misted with tears. "Well, um...Danny," she said, blinking away the tears and smiling, "congratulations to you and Loretta."

"Thank you, miss," he replied, shoving the last two suitcases into the overcrowded trunk. "We're real happy. Hope you and your guy will be, too."

"Yes," she whispered, turning her head to stare into space. "I hope we will be, too."

Ten minutes later, Martha was listening to Laurie's chatter while nervously waiting for Jake to arrive. "Oh, Martha!" Laurie squealed, when her friend stepped from the cab. "You look beautiful! Turn around. Let me look at you. Hey, I did a nice job on your hair, didn't I?"

"It's perfect," Martha murmured, craning her neck to look past Laurie to the waiting chambers of the justice of the peace. "Is Jake here yet?"

"No one's here but you and me."

"Oh, well," Martha said, glancing at her watch, "leave it to Jake Molloy to be late for his own wedding. I suppose we'll just have to sit and wait."

"Are you nervous?" Laurie inquired.

"Not even a tremor," Martha answered, holding out a steady hand. "I was nervous yesterday, but talking to Jake straightened me right out."

Laurie broke into a happy grin. "See what love will do?"

"Mmm," Martha murmured noncommittally. Only *she* could appreciate the humor of her situation, even if it was only black humor at best.

"Is that the elevator?" Laurie asked excitedly. "It is! Oh, look, it's Mr. Molloy and Dave Schneider." Laurie tugged at Martha's arm. "You didn't tell me Dave would be here," she whispered, then broke into a beaming smile. "Oh, look, Martha, isn't it wonderful?"

Martha could only stare. Jake and Dave Schneider were supervising two men in white coats who were rolling in a table covered with a white linen cloth, arrayed with silver serving trays and compotes. A huge bouquet of pink roses burst from a crystal vase. A bottle of champagne chilled in a silver ice bucket and a small mound of beluga caviar sat on a bed of crushed ice, surrounded by slices of lemon and chilled shrimp with cocktail sauce.

Jake brought out a small bouquet of white roses and baby's breath from behind his back and handed it to Martha. "I thought you should have flowers," he announced soberly.

Martha sat and stared up at him, not knowing what to say. Laurie nudged her. "Kiss him!" she whispered.

Feeling awkward, Martha stood up and hesitantly took the flowers. "They're beautiful," she murmured, holding them up to inhale their sweet scent. "I . . . I didn't expect anything like this."

"I thought it was the least I could do."

Martha's gaze flickered from Jake's. She felt a thrill of pleasure at the look of surprise on his face as he took in her new hairdo and elegant dress. Then a door opened and the justice of the peace arrived, saving Martha from having to comment further.

"Well, well," he said, beaming as he took in the linen-covered table. "What a nice touch. And which of you is the happy couple?"

Jake took Martha's hand, which was suddenly trembling. "We are," he replied. "Are you all right?" he whispered to her.

She could only nod. Her throat had suddenly closed up and she realized for the first time in her life what stage fright was. At least, she thought that was what it was.

"I know your plane leaves in a couple of hours, sir," the justice continued. "Your efficient secretary made a point of reminding me. We'll hurry along now so that you can all enjoy the pleasant repast you've so thoughtfully provided."

The ceremony went by in a blur. It was short and to the point, with the traditional wedding vows unceremoniously recited by Jake, then by Martha. She only heard two words—"I do"—when pronounced by Jake and later by herself.

Perhaps the fact that Jake had slipped a marvelous diamond-encrusted wedding band on her hand had momentarily startled her. She could tell he was also feeling a bit strange. She almost smiled at the look on his face when Jake held her hand after slipping on the wedding band. He seemed genuinely moved by the moment.

"Under the power invested in me as justice of the peace of the city of New York, I now pronounce you man and wife. You may kiss the bride, sir."

Before she knew what was happening, she was in Jake's arms. For a moment she went rigid, then she felt his lips on hers and everything went blank. An insistent buzzing took over her ears and sparks exploded behind her closed lids. She felt herself melting into Jake's embrace, experienced a strange heat enveloping her as she clung to him, her fingers clutched around the lapels of his jacket.

"Oh, Jake," she breathed unsteadily when he raised his lips from hers. "Jake..." She put a hand to her head and tried to steady herself. She felt dizzy, as if she'd just stepped off a ferris wheel.

But then Laurie was hugging and kissing her, and Dave Schneider took her into his arms and kissed her soundly while Laurie kissed Jake. In the happy chaos of the moment, her senses slowly returned. She only felt a momentary relapse when Jake looked into her eyes as he poured her champagne.

"To the bride," he toasted solemnly, then leaned forward and whispered in her ear, "Keep up the good work. You're quite the little actress."

She ducked her head and sipped at her champagne, trying to regain her composure. Somehow she had to keep Jake from realizing that she hadn't been acting. His kiss had literally swept her off her feet, as had the rest of the ceremony. She'd thought it would be cold, sterile and businesslike, but Jake had turned the tables on her. What else, she wondered vaguely, might he surprise her with?

"Caviar?" he offered, holding out a small bit on a cracker.

"I... I've never had it before," she replied, angry at herself for stumbling over her words.

"Then perhaps this is the time to start."

She took the cracker and nibbled at it. "Ugh," she said, wrinkling her nose. "It's horrible! Why does everyone make such a fuss about it?"

"It's an acquired taste, I believe," Jake explained, munching on a cracker piled high with the stuff. "Funny, I'd have expected you to have had it every night for din-din, coming from your background."

She grabbed a shrimp and devoured it, wishing she were cool and cosmopolitan. "Mother and Dad liked it, but I never tried it. I thought it looked rather gross." She peered at it, making a face. "Matter of fact, I still do."

Jake grinned and helped himself to more caviar. "More champagne, then?"

"No, I really shouldn't. I'm quite dizzy as it is."

"Oh? All this getting to you, is it?"

She glanced at him and saw that he was enjoying her discomfort immensely. That riled her. She decided it was time she turned a few tables herself. Daringly she put her arm through his and went up on tiptoe and kissed him. His lips, she realized, were amazingly soft and utterly delicious. She knew it was only the champagne that was giving her the courage to act so outrageously, but she figured she should take advantage of it while she could.

"Guess what?" she murmured, feeling dizzy again. "I discovered there's one way I do like caviar."

"Oh?"

She nuzzled his cheek. "Mm," she murmured. "On you."

Jake went rigid from surprise, but recovered quickly. He put his arm around her and drew her close. "Then perhaps we should bring it along in the cab."

"Actually," she said, suddenly sobering up, "I think we should bring the champagne along."

"Reduces your inhibitions, eh?" Jake remarked, chuckling.

She glared at him and took a healthy swig. "Just makes the thought of spending three weeks alone with you a little more bearable, that's all," she told him under her breath.

"Why, darling," Jake replied, loudly enough so that Dave and Laurie could hear, "That's the most wonderful thing you've ever suggested." He bent and kissed her and she felt herself turn to mush. She wasn't acting now—this was pure, instinctive lust. She returned Jake's kiss measure for measure, glorying in the pleasurable feelings that spilled through her, like water rushing in a brook.

"Uh-*hum*!" Dave Schneider said, clearing his throat loudly. "I think it's time you two left—if you want to catch your plane, that is."

Reluctantly Martha let go of Jake, still feeling pleasantly dazed. Laurie hooked an arm through hers and strolled with her toward the elevator.

"You two look wonderful together," Laurie murmured, hugging her. "Have a great time in Puerto Rico."

"We're not going to Puerto Rico," Martha corrected without thinking.

"Oh? I thought that's where you said you were going."

Martha shook her head. "We're flying there to catch a plane to St. Matthew's." Then she realized what she'd said and turned to Laurie, stricken by having spilled her and Jake's secret. "But you can't tell anyone, not even my parents," she whispered fiercely. "They'd kill me, and I don't want that. Promise me you won't tell."

"Why? What's the big deal?" Laurie's face took on a knowing look. "Oh, I'll bet Jake's going down there to give Bert Taylor hell about the work delays, isn't he?"

"Laurie, if you say a word to anyone I'll never speak to you again and Jake will fire you."

"Okay, okay! My gosh, you'd think it was a big secret. Everyone in the organization knows Bert's head is on the line with this one."

"I don't care what everyone knows. I only care about you being quiet about this. You're not to tell a single soul."

Laurie shrugged. "Doesn't Dave know?"

"No one knows," Martha answered, thinking fast to come up with a reasonable excuse. "This is our honeymoon. We don't want Bert to find out we'll be on the island or he'll be bugging Jake every minute. Jake didn't even want to go to St. Matthew's for our honeymoon, but he kept telling me how beautiful it is, that I begged him to take me there and he finally agreed. So you have to keep this thing quiet or it's on both our heads."

"Hey, look, my lips are sealed," Laurie promised, grinning. "I won't even mention it to my cat."

"Good. Just see that you don't."

"Oh, I think it's so exciting that you convinced him to go to St. Matthew's. I mean, it's so romantic, like him turning up here with the flowers and champagne and all. Anyone can see you're crazy about each other. I just can't figure out how you two kept it such a secret at work. I swear, no one even suspects."

"Keep it that way. We don't want anyone to know till we get back. It was...er...kind of a snap decision on our part. We'd like some time alone to...um...you know...really get to know each other...."

"Sure, I understand," Laurie said, giggling. "Oh, I just know you're going to have a wonderful honeymoon."

Impulsively Martha hugged her. "Thanks for everything. Keep my office out of trouble, will you?"

"Everything will be fine. Just go and have a good time and forget all about work."

Martha hid a bleak grin. This whole thing was about work, but then no one knew that but Jake and herself. When the elevator door opened, Jake took her arm and escorted her inside. Martha looked back at Laurie, suddenly needing her support. "Aren't you coming?"

"No, I'll stay here with Dave and help clean up the food and stuff." Laurie blew her a kiss. "Have a great time, you two. See you in three weeks."

The doors slid shut, closing Martha up with Jake. "Well!" she said, springing as far away from him as she could. "That went really great."

"You don't look like yourself," Jake remarked.

She stared at him. "What?"

He pointed at her. "Your hair. It's different. And that dress..."

She looked down at herself. "You told me to go shopping, Jake. Don't you like it?" she asked, feeling suddenly let down.

"I like it—I'm just not used to it," he said, then hurriedly consulted his watch. "I hope you told that cab to wait. We're cutting it close to get to the airport on time."

"He'll wait," Martha told him confidently.

"Ah, the old Martha—refreshingly sure of herself, the completely efficient right-hand man."

"Did you think I'd turn into a flibbertygibbet once I took the wedding vows?" she asked dryly.

"No, but I have to admit you surprised me."

"Oh?"

"Yes, you—" He broke off, frowning as he considered her, then he shrugged as the elevator doors opened. "Oh, well, here we are. And there's the cab! You must have given him a fifty to wait this long."

"No, I merely treated him like a human being. No money changed hands, no palms were greased. And will you please act like you're happy? Danny believes in marriage. I wouldn't want to disappoint him if he found out that this is just a business arrangement."

"Danny? On a first-name basis, are we?"

"Yes," she said, smiling sweetly, "we are."

"Hey," Danny shouted, jumping out of the cab, "this the happy groom?"

"This is he," Martha answered, beaming at the driver. "Danny, meet my husband, Jake Molloy. Jake, this is Danny."

"Hey, my man," Danny said, slapping Jake's hand in a high five greeting. "You're a lucky fella. Martha's a great gal. I think you're gonna be real happy, you know. I feel it here—" he tapped his stomach "—right in the ol' gut."

Jake nodded, looking slightly rattled by the exchange. He met Martha's amused gaze over Danny's head, then returned the cabbie's hearty handshake. "I'm sure we'll be very happy, too."

"Yeah, well, you two lovebirds get in. We're startin' to run a little late, you know? But I'll get you there. If anyone can, ol' Danny DeGennaro can."

"I'm glad to hear that," Jake answered, settling in the back seat next to Martha. "If you get us there with time to spare, there's a hundred in it for you."

"Hey! A little incentive, eh?" Danny replied, slapping the car into gear and taking off with a squeal of tires and cloud of exhaust smoke. "Hold on, guys and gals. Ol' Danny's in the driver's seat!"

It was safer, Martha found, to forget exactly who was in the driver's seat, or that they were even in a cab. Danny drove the way the Texas Rangers used to ride—hard and wild. Even among New York's finest cabdrivers, Danny stood out.

"Well, you really pick 'em, sweetheart," Jake remarked, grinning at the expression on her face.

"Yes, but look at it this way," she said. "If he keeps driving like this, we'll get there two hours ago."

Jake chuckled. "Yeah, he does kind of have a way of making the clock go backward."

"You two awright back there?" Danny shouted as he good-naturedly shook his fist at another driver.

"We're just fine," Martha said musically.

"I don't see you kissing," came Danny's singsong voice as he peered into the rearview mirror and just missed a truck.

"We'd kiss," Martha explained, "if you'd just keep your eyes on the road."

"Oh! I get it! You guys want a little privacy."

"Exactly," Martha acknowledged, taking a relieved breath as Danny turned back to the wheel and managed to keep from sideswiping another cab.

"Well?" Danny demanded. "You two kissing yet?"

"Kiss me, dammit," Martha whispered urgently, "or he'll have us in the hospital in traction in two minutes."

Chuckling, Jake took her in his arms. "My lovely wife," he murmured, grinning at her. "If you think Danny drives crazy, wait till you see the cabs on St. Matthew's."

"Oh? Are they this bad?"

"This *bad*?" Jake asked, laughing out loud. "Honey, the cabs on St. Matthew's make this look like a silver stretch limo with velvet upholstery. And the drivers—"

"Are you kissing back there yet?" Danny shouted happily, swerving to avoid hitting a bus.

"Good Godfrey," Martha muttered angrily. "Will you please kiss me before that madman manages to get us both killed?"

"Hey, he's *your* friend, not mine. All it takes is treating him like a decent human being. At least I believe that's what you said."

"Shut up and kiss me," Martha demanded, wrenching his head down and planting a kiss on his mouth.

"Sweetheart, that's not how you do it," Jake said, laughing when Martha went up for air. "Kissing is an art, perfected with much practice in a slow, leisurely, drawn-out manner."

"If we drew it out much longer we'd end up in a morgue," Martha snapped, then dived into Jake's arms again when Danny shouted an obscenity at a police car. "Oh, God—" she clung to Jake "—he's going to get us killed. I knew this marriage was jinxed. I just knew it."

"My Lord, that's right," Jake said. "We forgot to kill a chicken at the ceremony."

"You can make jokes all you want, Jake Molloy, but this isn't funny."

"Why are you so godawful nervous?" Jake demanded. "Granted, Danny's driving is the worst I've ever seen, but only by a hair."

"Oh, Jake," she pleaded, leaning back and putting a hand to her nervous stomach. "It isn't only Danny's driving. I'm thinking ahead, to the airport."

"What's so bad about that?"

"I'm terrified of flying."

"I see," Jake replied, unable to keep his lips from twitching in amusement. "Well, consider it this way—we can't have a pilot who's half as bad as Danny, and once we get off the ground, there won't be anyone around for miles to hit."

"Why doesn't that comfort me?"

"My dear wife," Jake said, taking her hand. "You're a married woman now. You have a husband to take care of you. Just hold my hand and drink a lot and you'll be just fine."

"If I make it through the next few hours, I'll be fine the rest of my life. Nothing else will ever be able to faze me."

"Not even the prospect of our wedding night?"

"Oh, Lord," she moaned, sliding down in the seat and trying to disappear. "Why did you even have to mention it? I swear to you, if you even so much as look at me tonight, I'll bean you with a coconut."

"Well, at least I have you thinking beyond the airplane flight," Jake observed contentedly.

"Jake, did you bring the champagne?"

"No, sweetheart. I forgot all about it. Why? Are you having second thoughts about our marriage?"

"Actually, I'm wondering why I ever even had first thoughts. What was wrong with me to let you talk me into an insane thing like this? I must be crazy. *You* must be crazy."

"Well, if I'm not now, I sure will be within a few days," Jake remarked dryly.

"What was that supposed to mean?" Martha asked.

"Are we still kissing back there?" Danny called out, leaning on his horn and slamming his foot on the brake to avoid going through the back end of a truck.

"Oh, Lord," Martha repeated, sliding farther down into her seat. She wished she had a big hat to pull over her head. "Just get me through this," she prayed out loud. "Please just get me through this."

Chuckling again, Jake patted her hand. "Actually, I think this might turn out to be fun."

"Fun?" she retorted, staring at him as if he were mad. "You think this is *fun*?"

"Well, so far it has been," he said, shrugging innocently.

"You are sick, Jake Molloy," she concluded, closing her eyes and wishing she had a dozen aspirin.

Grinning, Jake looked out the window. "Hang on, honey. Airport's straight ahead."

"Great," she responded bleakly, staring at the impressive snarl of traffic that jammed the entrance to JFK. There was no going back now, she realized. This time, she had well and truly gotten herself mixed up in a certifiable adventure. She just hoped she would live to talk about it.

Four

———

Martha sat in the plane, her fingers locked on the arms of the seat.

"Haven't you ever flown before?" Jake asked.

"Never."

"Well, as soon as we take off, I'll have the stewardess bring you a stiff drink. You'll find out that flying is like sitting in a giant cocktail lounge, five thousand miles off the ground."

"Did you have to mention the exact altitude? That's the part I'm afraid of. I don't think God ever intended man to get more than ten feet off the ground."

"Explain skyscrapers and elevators, then," Jake suggested.

"Skyscrapers and elevators are attached to the ground, but a plane actually leaves it."

"I'm sorry this is a matter of such grave concern to you."

"That's really not funny, Jake."

"What?" he asked.

"You mentioned graves. Under these particular circumstances, I'd appreciate it if you'd keep your puns to yourself."

Resting his elbow on the arm of the seat, Jake put his chin in his hand and stared at her. "I can't believe this is you. I've worked with you for five years and I've never seen you lose it once until today."

"Lose what? My cool or my lunch? You'll probably see me do both within the hour."

"Uh-uh," he said, one corner of his mouth turning up in amusement. "Not Martha Simmons—excuse me, Martha Molloy."

"Oh, God, now I'm *really* feeling ill."

"Just the mention of your new name does it to you, eh?"

She nodded bleakly. "Here we are, going to some uncivilized island where we're expected to act like happy newlyweds, when all the while we're actually investigating people who practice voodoo on live birds. Face it, Jake. This is a voyage to hell. Nothing will go right. I feel it in my bones."

"Well, those are certainly encouraging words," he commented dryly. "Remind me to rent you a video of *It's a Wonderful Life*. You could use a shot of optimism."

"Jake, what I could use is a shot of whiskey."

"Buckle your seat belt, honey," he said, grinning at her. "We're about to take off."

"What about my whiskey?"

"That comes once we're up in the air."

"But what if we don't get up in the air?"

"Then you won't need it."

"Oh, Lord," she groaned, putting a hand to her head. "Why do you always have an answer for everything?"

"Why do you always have a question? Just sit back and relax. You're gonna love flying."

"Jake, I am not a bird. I will not love flying, I—" She broke off when the plane began to back up. "Omigod, we're moving."

"Yes, but take comfort—we're still on the ground."

"Why are we going backward? Jake, this doesn't feel right. Shouldn't we be going forward?"

"All in good time."

She gave him a hard look, then froze as the plane lurched forward and began moving slowly down the runway. "We're never going to get off the ground this way," she remarked, closing her eyes. "Even I know that you have to get up a little speed."

"We're merely approaching our runway. There are literally miles of runways out here, and we'll probably have to wait quite a while for other planes to take off and land before it's our turn. Now sit back and relax before I chloroform you."

"If only you would," she said forlornly, staring out the window. Her stomach was unsettled, her heart was thumping madly and her palms were clammy, yet Jake sat next to her yawning as he leafed through a magazine. Why was there no justice in this life?

Somehow the moments ticked by. At last they were ready to take off. The engines revved and the pilot's voice crackled over the intercom—"Ladies and gentlemen, prepare for takeoff."

Suddenly the plane was hurtling down the runway and Martha, her eyes squeezed shut, was clutching Jake's hand. There was a strange lift and she realized they were off the ground. She experienced a momentary spasm of terror, then intense relief. They were up. There was no turning back now, she told herself, her practicality returning at last.

"Feeling better?" Jake asked.

"A little."

"There. That wasn't so bad, was it?"

"I could still use a drink," she murmured faintly.

"Are you sure you want a drink? They've probably got some motion-sickness pills on board."

"No, it was just nerves. I'm feeling much better now, but I'd like to take the edge off, if you don't mind."

"Fine with me. Stewardess? Could you bring my wife a drink, please? She's a bit of an unhappy camper right now."

"What can I get you, ma'am?"

"Whiskey would be good. And lots of it," Martha said with a wobbly smile.

Two minutes later, Martha had downed a shot of straight whiskey. It joined the champagne she'd had earlier and sent a message all in capital letters to her brain: RELAX. She yawned delicately and rested her head against the seat.

Moments later, she was asleep, dreaming that she was a little gray wren flapping her pitiful wings in the limitless blue sky. Then the dream changed. As if by magic, she turned into a beautiful sea gull soaring gracefully over a fog-shrouded tropical island while being pursued by a magnificent eagle. But the eagle didn't frighten her; he looked just like Jake Molloy....

They changed planes in Puerto Rico, where Martha had her first glimpse of palm trees swaying in humid semitropical breezes. She wanted to gaze blissfully at the sight and take time to study the hordes of people milling around the airport, but Jake took her hand and hustled her through the maze of busy concourses where the lilting sounds of Spanish blended with English. They raced by mothers with crying babies and senior citizens who hobbled along behind lackadaisical redcaps. They skirted trolleys piled high with baggage and pushed their way through crowds of passengers deplaning. At last they arrived at the gate where the small commuter airline waited to take them and seven other people to St. Matthew's.

"Good grief," Martha exclaimed when she spied the small plane. "We're going over the ocean in *that*?"

"We won't be in it very long," Jake reassured her. "It's a short hop to St. Matthew's from here. The stewardess will no sooner have served drinks than we'll be fastening our seat belts, getting ready to land."

"Well, I suppose that's a consolation," she replied, then decided to distract herself as they waited to board the plane by studying their fellow passengers.

An elderly man with a florid face and a rounded belly stood next to them. Dressed in a white suit and wearing a straw hat, he looked as if he'd stepped out of a Graham Greene novel. When he spoke to the woman with him in a pronounced English accent, Martha grinned to herself. He sounded just as she'd imagined he would—like the stereotypical retired British Army colonel on vacation in the islands.

But where he was red-faced and overweight, his wife was pale and angular. She wore white gloves and a flowered dress and looked as if she were going to high tea at Buckingham Palace. Rigid gray curls surrounded her long face but in no way softened it. Her profile seemed hacked from marble. As a young woman she must have been lovely, with the pale, soft skin of an Englishwoman. Now she seemed remote and unfriendly, with her pointed nose perpetually held in the air.

The other passengers included a dark-skinned man who wore a suit and carried a briefcase. He seemed intent on reading a report and looked as if flying out of Puerto Rico to a Caribbean island were an everyday occurrence. Martha peered at him speculatively, wondering what kind of business he might be doing on St. Matthew's. The remaining passengers were two young couples, both obviously on their honeymoons. They hung on to their partners adoringly and had eyes only for each other. Watching them, Martha realized that she and Jake weren't acting as if they were in love.

"Jake," she whispered, tugging on his arm. He was reading a magazine article and not paying the slightest attention to her.

"Mmm?"

"Put your arm around me."

"Why?" he asked, still immersed in reading the article.

"Look at those other couples. They look like they're on their honeymoon. We don't."

Jake looked up and followed her gaze, taking in the two young couples fawning over their partners. Grunting, he closed the magazine and put his arm around her. "Well," he murmured, his mouth near her ear, "I guess you're right. If we're going to pull this off, we'd better start acting the part. Bat your eyelashes at me, Martha. Act like you're dying to get me alone."

She looked at him balefully. "I've never batted my lashes in my life. What makes you think I can start now?"

"This," he answered, lowering his mouth and kissing her.

Taken by surprise, her first impulse was to push him away, but then something strange happened—she forgot everything and just responded. It was a dazzling kiss, filled with passion and heat, making her heart race and her pulses pound. She found herself slipping into a state of increased excitement when Jake pulled away.

"Didn't I tell you?" he said. "It's the old Molloy Magic."

"Jake," she murmured, gazing adoringly into his eyes, "if we weren't in public, I'd laugh in your face."

"Oh, would you now?" he challenged, grinning. "You mean to tell me a woman who's never batted her lashes at a man in her life can just turn on a response like that at the drop of a hat?"

She shrugged. "Why not? You obviously did."

He shook his head. "I don't buy it, Martha. You're falling under the spell of old Molloy already, but you just won't admit it."

"And you won't admit you're full of hot air," she retorted, pulling out of his arms and tossing her head disdainfully.

"Now, Martha, if we're not careful, people will think we're having a lovers' spat."

"Let them" she said under her breath.

"Martha, you're not cooperating."

"Maybe we'd better get one thing straight right now. We're acting, Jake. Don't let that male ego of yours begin to get any bright ideas. I'm not falling for you. Nor will I. Is that clear?"

"You almost make it a challenge," he remarked lazily.

"The only challenge, as far as I'm concerned," she stated, her voice rising slightly, "is putting up with you for the next three weeks."

"Ah-*hum*!"

Martha and Jake looked up to find the elderly British man watching them with twinkling eyes. "I'm sorry I overheard just now, but it appears you're having a bit of a lovers' quarrel." He shook his head, his eyes closed admonishingly. "It won't do. Not on your honeymoon. It *is* your honeymoon, isn't it?"

"Why, yes," Martha replied, her cheeks growing pink. "But how could you tell?"

"I saw you kissing a moment ago." The old man chuckled. "I may be old, but I'm not blind. What I saw was two young people very attracted to each other, but still in love with the chase. But you see, you're married now. It's time to give up the petty quarrels and forge a bond."

"Oliver!"

The elderly man turned and spied his wife descending on him, her face a picture of displeasure. "Harriet," he said jovially, "come meet this splendid young couple. I was giving them some fatherly advice."

"I'm sure they don't need advice, Oliver," she corrected sternly, then turned to Martha and Jake and smiled coolly.

"I'm Harriet Thumpwhistle, and this is Oliver, my husband. You'll have to pardon him. He has a penchant for getting involved where he doesn't belong."

"But I think he's charming," Martha protested, smiling at Oliver, who beamed at her. "I'm Martha Sim—Oh, Lord, I almost forgot," she exclaimed, again growing pink. "I'm married now, aren't I?" She looked at Jake and noted the gleam in his eye. "I'm Martha, and this is Jake Molloy. We're on our honeymoon."

"You'll love St. Matthew's," Harriet Thumpwhistle enthused. "Oliver and I go there every year, don't we, Oliver?"

"Yes, my dear, we do," he responded, then turned to Jake. "Where are you staying?"

"The Paradise," Jake answered.

Oliver's florid face grew even more red with pleasure. "Splendid!" he boomed. "Absolutely splendid! That's where we're staying! We've been going there for years. It's by far the nicest hotel on the island."

"Not for long," the dark-skinned man in the business suit interjected. "I hear they're building a Hilliard Hotel on St. Matthew's."

Startled, Martha turned to the stranger who had evidently been listening to their conversation. For some reason, she didn't like him. There was something sneaky about him. Anyone who listened in on private conversations couldn't be trusted.... But then Oliver had listened in on hers and Jake's, she remembered, and she turned back to gaze at the elderly British gentleman more closely.

"You can't be serious!" Oliver Thumpwhistle exclaimed, his face now scarlet. "Building a Hilliard on St. Matthew's! That's monstrous. It'll destroy the island, turn it into a regular tourist haunt. Good Lord, before you know it, they'll have American fast-food chains there, too!"

"Is St. Matthew's so undeveloped then?" Martha asked innocently, throwing a quick look at Jake, who looked amazingly disinterested in the entire conversation.

"It's totally unspoiled," Oliver explained. "There are only three hotels on the entire island, and they're all rather small in comparison to a Hilliard. No fancy gambling casinos or indoor swimming pools, just good service and the same friendly faces year after year."

"It sounds lovely," Martha said. "I can see why you're upset about a Hilliard being built."

"Yes," Oliver added, huffing and puffing in his agitation. "It's this blasted so-called progress I can't stand, you see. Harriet and I have come to St. Matthew's for years to get away from commercialization. If they let Hilliard build, the other large chains will be right behind them. Dammit, they're going to ruin St. Matthew's!" He wiped the sweat off his forehead. "Lord, what will they think up next?"

"I'm sure the Hilliard will respect the ambience of the island and not turn it into a three-ring circus," the dark-skinned man again interrupted.

Jake gave him a quick look. "I hope you're right," he said, taking Martha by the arm. "But we can't solve all the world's problems right now. They're ready for us to board."

"What do you make of all this?" Martha whispered as they stepped into the small plane.

Jake shrugged noncommittally. "Who can tell? There's one thing I'll look into right away, though."

"What's that?"

"The identity of our friend in the suit. It's interesting that he knows a Hilliard is being built. He even came to its defense, in a manner of speaking."

"Do you think he could be involved in delaying the construction?"

"My dear, I think any one of them could be involved in it. That's why it'll behoove us to keep our heads on straight and remember to act like we know nothing about Hilliard Hotels—or any hotel, for that matter.''

"Play dumb, you mean."

Jake smiled grimly. "Precisely."

Half an hour later, the plane began its descent to St. Matthew's. Martha gazed out the window, enraptured by her first sight of the island. It was relatively small, covered in dense, dark green vegetation. Low, rounded hills sloped gently toward turquoise waters that sparkled beneath a brilliant sun and washed up in lacy waves on immaculate white beaches. Here and there, red-tiled roofs peeked out from the dark trees. But for the most part, the island seemed uninhabited.

"It looks beautiful," she murmured, turning to Jake, who was peering down at the island as they approached it.

"Wait till you're on the ground," he said. "It will take your breath away. I was only here for a short visit when I purchased the land for the hotel site, but what little I saw of the island convinced me it's the most beautiful in the Caribbean."

Jake was right. When Martha stepped off the plane, she felt the cool trade winds, smelled the sweet scents of flowering bushes and shrubs, and knew she had indeed stumbled into a tropical paradise. They piled their luggage into an open-topped truck and slid in next to the driver, a handsome black man with a wide grin filled with huge white teeth. He wore cut-off jeans and a New York Yankees T-shirt. Civilization evidently extended this far, Martha thought in amusement, though one couldn't prove it by the unspoiled landscape.

"The Paradise, it is a very nice hotel," the man commented, introducing himself as Jimmy. His voice was low and musical, lilting in the soft, musical cadences that characterized the islanders' speech.

"We hear there are only two other hotels on the island," Martha said.

"Yes. For over fifty years, there have only been three hotels here—the Paradise, the Lost Lagoon and Pelican Perch. It stay that way another fifty years, too."

Startled, Martha looked at Jake, whose face showed no emotion. "But I thought I heard Hilliard Hotels was building a hotel here," she remarked.

"They buy the land," Jimmy replied, grinning, "but they not build the hotel."

"Why not?"

Jimmy shrugged, careening around a hairpin curve and forcing Martha to grab onto Jake. "The gods, they not happy. The gods not let another hotel be built here."

"The gods?" Martha repeated faintly, trying to suppress a nervous shiver.

"Yes, the ancient gods who lived on this island before man came. They not like progress. They wish man to live in peace and harmony. They say life should be peaceful, not filled with honking horns and traffic lights and rush hours like in New York City."

"You've been to New York?" Martha asked in surprise.

"Oh, yes, I go once. I stay a week. See a Yankees game," he said, grinning as he pointed to his T-shirt. "But I come back. Didn't like the *noise*!" He made a face and pressed his hands to his ears.

Martha stared at a goat that was ambling across the road. She felt a sense of déjà vu, as if she were back in Danny DeGrennaro's cab, only transported to an uncivilized land. "Jimmy, there's a goat up ahead!" she shrieked. "Don't you think you should put your hands back on the steering wheel?"

Jimmy grinned. "Everyone worry about Jimmy drives, but Jimmy never once have an accident. And the goats, they have a right to cross the road, too."

"Yes, but—" Martha clamped her mouth shut as Jimmy shot past the goat, who looked up while munching peacefully on a clump of grass.

"You see?" Jimmy laughed. "The goat, he is a sacred animal. All animals sacred on St. Matthew's."

"Even chickens?" Martha asked before she could stop herself.

"Especially chickens."

Martha looked at Jake, who was grinning at her. She tossed her head and fastened her eyes back on the road. Jimmy continued to race up hills, and over narrow stretches of road bounded by dense vegetation where tropical birds called eerily. At one point in their journey to the hotel, the passed a waterfall cascading over glistening rocks, surrounded by pink flamingos and brilliant bursts of pink and red flowers amid the surrounding dark green trees and shrubs.

"Why, those flowers looked like poinsettias!" Martha exclaimed.

"They are poinsettias," Jimmy said matter-of-factly.

"But I thought they only bloomed at Christmas."

"Here, they bloom all year," Jimmy replied, smiling. "The gods, they favor us with the most beautiful flowers in the world."

He had no sooner finished speaking when he rounded a curve and slowed down. Up ahead, a palatial white house emerged from the surrounding junglelike growth. Balconies with wrought-iron filigree railings jutted from its sides. French doors led to the balconies and stone patios on the ground floor. Lush tropical vegetation surged toward the building, held back by meticulous gardening. Huge dark-timbered wooden doors stood open at the front entrance, inviting guests to enter.

"Welcome to Paradise," Jimmy said, pulling the truck to a stop and cutting the engine.

Martha stared at the hotel in awe. They had reached their final destination at last—Paradise.

FIVE

An hour later, Martha had unpacked her bags and changed into a sleeveless white blouse and linen shorts. Jake had left the room immediately after he'd unpacked, saying he wanted to look around the hotel. She found him seated on the back terrace, a drink in hand as he talked with Oliver and Harriet Thumpwhistle and a tall, handsome man with blond hair and a full moustache.

"Sweetheart," Jake said as he rose and kissed her. "You already know Oliver and Harriet. This is Sidney Howell. He's the manager of the Paradise."

To her surprise, Sidney took her hand and raised it to his lips. "Mrs. Molloy, how nice to meet you."

She smiled automatically. Sidney Howell was extraordinarily good-looking, she realized, now that she was seeing him up close. And the admiration that glowed in his eyes as he looked at her told her he found her attractive. She felt an unfamiliar thrill of delight. She was unused to even being noticed by men. Now she had two of them paying her court.

She glanced sardonically at Jake. Of course, one of them was doing it with ulterior motives in mind, but it was pleasurable all the same.

"It's very nice to meet you, Mr. Howell," she responded, smiling as she took a seat next to Jake. "Your hotel is charming. Oliver and Harriet told us earlier that they've been coming here for years."

Sidney darted an amused glance at the elderly couple. "Yes, well...Oliver and Harriet visit dozens of hotels in the Caribbean, but on St. Matthew's, the Paradise is their home. But can I get you a drink, Mrs. Molloy? Some white wine perhaps, or would you prefer an island cooler?"

Martha looked out at the wide path that had been hacked through the foliage surrounding the hotel. "I'd love a drink, but then I want to follow that path. I saw it from the balcony upstairs. Where does it lead? To Shangri-la?"

"Actually," Sidney said, "we're surprisingly close to the beach. You follow the path through the garden a short distance, then you'll come to an old set of wooden steps. They take you down to the private beach. I'd be glad to send your drink down there to you if you and your husband would like to explore a bit."

"That sounds wonderful," Jake enthused, taking her by the hand. "Come along, darling, I want you to myself for a while."

"But what shall I send to you?" Sidney called after them. "Wine? A piña colada? A daiquiri?"

"A piña colada sounds wonderful," Martha called back over her shoulder, laughing as she fell into step beside Jake. She glanced at her new husband ironically. "Is this part of the act?"

"Not at all," he replied. "I wanted to speak with you privately. The beach seems the perfect place. I think perhaps I should tell you about my one and only visit to St. Matthew's. I came on a private plane and rented a villa on the other side of the island. A car was waiting for me, reserved in the real-estate agent's name. I drove myself to the villa. The only person on the island I had any contact with at all was the agent, Mr. Parsons. He's our one weak link. If we should happen upon him, he'd blow my cover immediately."

"*Now* you tell me!" Martha said.

"I didn't want to alarm you. I don't think there's much of a chance we'll run into Parsons, but he does know I chose the site for the new Hilliard hotel."

"Why don't you contact him and ask him to keep quiet about knowing you?" Martha said.

Jake frowned. "I'm not sure that's a good idea. On an island as small as this, one never knows whose side someone is on. Parsons is better kept out of the picture completely, I think. The trouble is, he may show up any time for a drink here at the hotel. Howell was telling me the Paradise is a favorite watering hole with the local businessmen."

"Great. Just what we need—a fly in the ointment already."

"Perhaps not. We'll have to wait and see. I just wanted to warn you in case you stumble on him."

"What should I do?" Martha inquired. "Play stupid?"

Jake grinned. "Despite my joke about playing dumb earlier, you couldn't play stupid if you wanted to. No, I don't think there'd be any problem if you met him. There are plenty of Molloys in the world, after all, so he probably wouldn't associate you with me. If you should happen to meet him, though, keep your ears open. Maybe he knows something about what's going on up at the construction site. His office is on the other side of the island. He's closer to the building site there, so he may mention it. The only danger is if he spots me and says something before I have a chance to speak to him."

"What would you say?"

"I suppose I'd have to ask him to be quiet for a while, and trust he'd play along."

"Mmm," Martha responded, smiling slightly. "But trust isn't your long suit, is it, Mr. Molloy?"

"Let's just say I didn't get to be vice president for hotel development by taking everyone at face value."

"So, what do you think of everyone so far?"

"Who knows? They could all be innocent, or any one of them could have a motive for wanting to keep Hilliard Hotels off the island. Howell might be afraid the competition would hurt business and endanger his job. The dark-skinned man on the plane could be associated with one of the other hotels on the islands. Parsons might have collected his real-estate commission, but he might hope to collect it again by forcing Hilliard to resell the land because building a hotel could prove to be impossible—"

"Surely you can't think that?" Martha said.

"Why not? He could make a tidy profit off selling the same piece of land over and over again to unsuspecting developers."

"And I suppose you even mistrust the Thumpwhistles."

"Sure. Old Oliver is a charmer, but he spoke vehemently against Hilliard when he found out we were building here."

"But surely that alone lets him off the hook!" Martha cried. "He didn't even know about Hilliard's building a hotel until that man on the plane told him."

"That's true," Jake agreed, then looked back over his shoulder and put an arm around Martha. "Don't look now, darling, but Jimmy is bringing us our drinks. Let's make it look like we're out here for more than the view."

Jake drew her into his arms and lowered his lips to hers. She felt the now familiar sensations shake her. But she also dimly noticed that it was growing easier and easier to respond to Jake. Kissing him was becoming almost second nature. Unwillingly, she had to confess that she liked this part of her job immensely.

Not that she would ever admit it to Jake, she thought as he released her. She might like kissing Jake Molloy, but she was still his secretary, and once they returned to New York, their marriage would be annulled and life would return to normal. It wouldn't be too smart to develop a crush on the man she worked for.

Jimmy handed Jake their drinks, then spread out a colorful blanket on the clean white sand of the deserted beach. In the west, the sun was sinking, spreading a rainbow of colors over the sky and ocean. The world seemed painted in scarlet and mauve, with a gold haze enveloping the entire landscape.

"Enjoy your drinks," Jimmy told them, smiling. "And don't bother about the glasses or blanket. Just leave them here when you come back. I get them in the morning."

Martha sipped her drink, then took a deep breath and lay back on the striped blanket. "Who'd ever have thought this could happen to me?" she said softly, gazing at the palm trees that lined the beach. Turquoise waters lapped the pristine white sand, but farther out the water changed colors, becoming green, then an intense dark blue. "It's magnificent," she continued. "I can't believe it's still winter in New York."

"Mmm," Jake responded, resting on one elbow. "It's probably snowing. Rush hour will be in full swing." He grinned and turned to her. "Aren't you glad you're with me?"

"I'm glad I'm here," she answered, choosing her words carefully. "I'm not necessarily glad we're doing what we're doing."

"Pretending to be married, you mean? Or investigating the holdup on construction?"

"Both. I'm not really sure I'll be able to carry off acting like a newlywed, and I've been rather worried since you mentioned Parsons."

"Don't worry about Parsons," Jake said. "I'll take care of him. And as far as carrying off our act, I think you're doing splendidly. Don't you?"

Playing for time, she sat up and took a sip of her drink. "I suppose so," she admitted after a moment.

"You don't sound convinced."

She shrugged. How could she even discuss her fears of getting further involved with Jake? If she liked kissing him this much after only a few hours, what would it be like after three weeks?

"You're worried about all this physical contact, aren't you?" he ventured.

Stiffening, she put down her drink and forced herself to laugh. "Perhaps a little...."

"Then come here and let me show you how easy it is."

She looked at him. "I really don't think that's a good idea."

"It's a wonderful idea. Good Old Oliver and Harriet are on the ridge watching us. Let's show them we really are honeymooners."

She lay back on the blanket, feeling her heart begin to slam against her ribs. This was precisely what she didn't want, yet it seemed she had no choice in the matter. As she was debating what had to be done, Jake rolled over and took her in his arms.

"Kiss me," he said. "And make it look like you mean it."

She lay very still and let him kiss her, but she couldn't respond. She was too aware of being watched. She felt awkward, like a schoolgirl who'd never been kissed. She was stiff and unpliable, though a strange thrill of pleasure was beginning deep inside her, despite telling herself she couldn't enjoy what she was doing.

"Ah, Martha," Jake whispered as he teased her earlobe with his lips, "what must I do to make you respond, hmm? This?" He took her lobe in his teeth and tugged on it gently.

"Or this?" The tip of his tongue entered her ear, forcing a groan from deep in her throat.

"Oh, Jake," she whispered shakily. "Please don't do that...."

"No?" he murmured. "But I think it's exactly what you need."

"No, it's..." She put her hand on his shoulder to push him away, but he flicked his tongue across her ear again, causing a deep shudder to go through her entire body. Against her will, she found herself putting her arms around him, pulling him down on top of her.

"You like it, don't you?" he murmured.

She moved her head back and forth, her eyes closed tight in protest. "No, I..." He suckled on her earlobe causing deeper and stronger spasms to run through her. "Oh, yes," she whispered urgently. "Oh, Jake, yes...."

He moved his lips lightly over her skin, dropping soft kisses here and there, brushing his hand incessantly back and forth across her bare shoulder. She felt giddy with pleasure, engulfed by sensations so new and overwhelming she was frightened by their intensity.

"Maybe we should stop," she suggested.

"I don't think so," Jake replied, beginning to pull the pins from her hair.

"Jake," she protested softly. "You shouldn't."

"But I should," he said, dropping petal-soft kisses on her lips. "We want to convince them back at the hotel, don't we? What better way than to come back from the beach with our clothes disheveled and your hair all mussed?"

He threw the last of her hairpins on the blanket and combed through her fine hair with his hand. "It's like silk," he mused, watching as the platinum strands slipped between his fingers. "Like fine gold silken thread. And so soft. I hadn't realized your hair was so soft." He bent and dropped light kisses on her forehead, moving his lips into her hair and down toward her ear.

She inhaled sharply as his tongue again began a deep, slow, thorough invasion of her ear. The invasion sent sharp spasms of desire shooting through her body. She clung to Jake, moaning softly as pleasure cascaded over her. She began a slow exploration of the muscles of his arms and shoulders, then down his back, moving her hands slowly over the powerful curve that descended to his waist.

"There," Jake said, raising his head. "That wasn't so bad, was it?"

"Not bad," she whispered, looking up at him, her dilated pupils making her blue eyes seem enormous in the dusky twilight.

He reached out and traced his forefinger lightly down her cheek. "Perhaps we can have another lesson later."

"Was this a lesson, then?" she asked.

He looked at her closely. "Wasn't it?"

She shrugged and sat up. "I suppose so." Glancing up at the ridge, she saw that Oliver and Harriet had disappeared. "They're gone now. We can stop. Perhaps we should go back to the hotel. I'm getting rather hungry." Hurriedly she began to gather the hairpins that Jake had discarded on the blanket.

Jake rested on one elbow, looking up at her speculatively. One corner of his mouth curled up in a grin, then he rose to his feet. "All right, we'll have dinner. Then we'll make it an early night. It is our wedding night, after all. I'm sure people will expect us to disappear quickly."

She glanced at him but refused to respond. Right now she was feeling too shaky, too unsure of herself. Conflicting feelings burgeoned within her—feelings she would rather not examine too closely. It was enough that they were falling into their roles and beginning to feel comfortable with each other.

At least she believed she was comfortable; but the inner voice that wouldn't accept lies told her otherwise. She stared straight ahead as they walked along the deserted path back to the hotel. She was afraid to even look at Jake, much less to speak to him. Suddenly everything was awkward. The kisses back on the beach had been too intimate, had brought her too much pleasure for her to shake off their effects so soon.

By the time they reached the hotel, she was trembling with nervousness. The very idea of going to their room and dressing for dinner together was enough to make her freeze up. Suddenly she wanted nothing more than to escape to the safety of her own room. She didn't want to share anything with Jake—not a bed or a bathroom, not even a table for dinner.

"You're looking rather tense," Jake murmured, taking her hand and pulling her into the shadows of the terrace.

She took a shaky breath. "I'm afraid I am. I..." Her gaze flickered from his. "Actually, I'd like to have a few moments to myself while I shower and dress for dinner. Would you mind very much waiting down here for a while?"

Jake seemed to be reading her mind, but to her relief he didn't question her. He simply inclined his head. "I'll wait in the bar. How long shall I give you? An hour?"

"A half an hour should do. I . . . I'll wait for you in the room."

He escorted her into the hotel, then stood and watched as she walked across the lobby toward the stairs. Her golden hair curled softly around her shoulders. His eyes drifted down her trim figure, taking in her long, slim legs beneath the white linen Bermuda-length shorts.

"She's a lovely woman," Sidney Howell remarked from behind Jake. "And you're a very lucky man."

Turning, Jake looked closely at Sidney, then back at Martha as she disappeared up the stairs. "Yes," he said, thoughtfully. "Yes, I do believe I am...."

Martha luxuriated in the stinging spray of the hot shower, washing away her tension and momentarily forgetting everything but the sheer joy of hot water and a fat cake of sweet-smelling soap. As she turned this way and that beneath the spray, she forgot that she'd meant to hurry. Time slipped by and still she stayed in the shower, perhaps because of an unconscious wish not to have to face what was coming up. She was thunderstruck when the bathroom door opened and Jake's voice broke into her reverie.

"My God, woman, are you *still* in the shower?"

She froze, then crossed her arms over her breast and huddled in a far corner of the shower, as if somehow this would protect her from Jake if he should draw the curtain back.

"I . . . I forgot the time," she explained, turning off the shower and reaching awkwardly for a towel. "I'm sorry, I didn't mean to take so long."

Jake placed his shaving kit on the vanity and grabbed a towel. "I hope you left some hot water for me."

Martha stood in the tub, wrapped in the damp towel, biting her lip indecisively. What should she do? Wait for Jake to leave the bathroom? Or nonchalantly stroll past him, wrapped only in a scrap of terry cloth, acting as if she did this sort of thing every day of her life?

"Well?" asked Jake. "Are you waiting for me to join you?"

Her eyes widened in fear. "No! I . . . I . . ." She drew the curtain back a fraction and peered around it. "My clothes," she said, staring imploringly at him. "They're in the bedroom."

"Shall I bring them to you?"

She swallowed awkwardly, then shook her head and forced a smile. "No, that's all right. I'll get them."

A moment passed. Jake stood and waited, then sighed and leaned against the vanity. "My dear Martha, it seems we have a problem. I'd like to use the shower, but you seem to have grown very attached to it."

She closed her eyes and sank back behind the shower curtain, feeling hot color fill her face. "Oh, Lord," she murmured, her voice shaking. "Jake, this is terribly awkward for me. I'm sorry, but I just can't parade around in a towel in front of you. It's impossible."

"I see."

"I'm not sure that you do."

He considered that, then levered himself away from the vanity. "I think I have the answer," he replied. "Be right back."

She stood in the shower, feeling as foolish as she'd ever felt in her life. Why hadn't she just walked past him as if she'd never given his presence a thought? This was a million times more awkward now. She was making mountains out of molehills.

Jake came back, his robe in hand. "Here," he told her, handing it around the shower curtain. "Put my robe on."

"Oh, thank you," she responded, gratitude vibrating in her voice. "It was foolish of me, but I forgot to bring mine in here. I just wasn't thinking. At home I never use a robe, so naturally when I came in here to take a shower, I forgot to bring it."

She slid back the shower curtain and stepped out of the tub. She stood for a moment, wishing a magic door would open and take her from this place, but no such luck. There was Jake, arms folded across his muscular chest, leaning back against the vanity, his gray eyes traveling lazily down her slim figure, which was dwarfed by the immensity of his terry-cloth robe. She couldn't get away from him. He was here; she was here. They were stuck together, and would continue to be for the next three weeks.

When Jake's gaze fastened on her head, she blushed. She dragged off her pink plastic shower cap. Her hair fell from its confines, straggling around her shoulders. She knew she was a mess. Her makeup was washed off, leaving her face as shiny and red as a freshly scrubbed apple. Her hair was damp, and she looked like a waif huddled in his enormous robe.

"Well," she commented. "Here we are."

Jake's lips twitched in amusement. "Yes," he said. "Here we are. The question is, what are we going to do about it?"

She stared at him, nonplussed. What were they going to do about it? She shook her head. "I don't know what you mean."

"Well, we can obviously tiptoe around each other, feeling awkward and wishing we were a million miles apart, or we can decide this is an adventure and simply enjoy ourselves. I opt for the latter, but I can't speak for you."

"So this is what you call an adventure," she answered, recovering her composure. "All right, then," she continued, clutching Jake's robe to her neck and drawing herself up to her full height. "An adventure it will be."

Turning, she strolled regally toward the bathroom door. She almost made it, but at the last moment she tripped on the sash of the robe. Mortified, she glanced back and saw that he was trying to keep from laughing out loud.

"Oh, shut up," she said irritably, and slammed the door after her. From behind the barrier, Jake's laughter mocked her. If she ever recovered her sense of humor, she thought, she just might begin to enjoy this entire mess.

Six

―――

More champagne?"

Martha smiled and put her hand over her glass. "I couldn't, Jake. Everything was delicious, but I'm going to fall off my chair if I drink another drop."

"But that's the joy of having a husband around—I'll carry you to our room, so you don't have to worry about walking straight, or walking at all, for that matter."

Martha smiled and looked around the gracious dining room. There were a few other couples scattered about, but no one sat nearby. They were isolated in their own corner near French doors that led to a sheltered terrace. Outside, tree frogs high up in the dense vegetation made a pleasant background noise in counterpoint to the soft classical music that played within. Earlier, a soft rain had fallen for about five minutes. It had stopped as quickly as it had begun. Their waiter explained that this was common on the island—every night about dusk a gentle rain fell, washing off the dark green foliage and cleansing the island for another day.

"Some say it is the gods weeping," he said in his musical voice. "But on St. Matthew's Island, there is no reason to weep." He flashed them a brilliant grin and drifted away, leaving them alone again.

Now they sat and sipped the last of their champagne. Martha's earlier awkwardness had been relieved and she sat, completely relaxed, enjoying the ambience of the elegant dining room, where cedar beams bisected the white stucco cathedral ceiling, and white linen cloths covered the mahogany tables. Sterling glowed at each place setting, and Spode china graced the tabletops. Magnificent tropical blooms floated in cut-glass bowls in the centerpieces.

"There's dancing in the cocktail lounge," Jake remarked. "Would you like to have another drink there?"

She smiled. "If I had another drink, Mr. Molloy, you *would* have to carry me upstairs."

"And wouldn't *that* make people talk," he commented, smiling.

Suddenly she was nervous. "Well," she said at last, "I suppose we can't put it off any longer."

"Put what off?"

"Going upstairs, of course. As much as I'd like to avoid this part of the charade, I suppose I can't."

"My God, Martha, you make it sound like being sentenced to prison. You forget, it's not a life term—it's only three weeks. Anyway, you won't have to worry. I'll turn my back and be asleep in a minute. I only hope my snoring doesn't keep you awake."

"You snore?"

"I'm told I do. I've never heard it personally. I'm always asleep when I do it."

"Uh-huh. And I imagine one of your cute little dinner companions from other romantic evenings has been kind enough to inform you in the morning."

"You sound jealous. Good. That's how wives are supposed to sound."

"But I'm not your wife," she replied triumphantly.

"Oh, but you are," he insisted, even more triumphantly.

Astounded, she realized he was right. "Isn't that extraordinary," she said slowly. "You're right. I *am* your wife."

"How does it feel, now that it's finally hit you?"

"It feels strange," she admitted wonderingly. "I'm flabbergasted. I've been focusing so much on the fact that we're here for other purposes that I've completely forgotten that we are truly and validly married. For some reason, I've kept thinking that this is only a pretend marriage. But it's real, isn't it? Even if we don't intend to make it last."

"Oh, it's real, all right." Jake held up his champagne glass and studied the bubbles that floated to the top. Raising the glass to his lips, he swallowed the rest in one gulp. "That's why I think we shouldn't worry too much about what happens in the next three weeks."

"What do you mean?"

Jake set his glass down and raised his eyes to hers. "Simply that we have nothing to worry about. We're legally married."

She stared at him, unable to figure out what he was saying. "I'm afraid I don't know what you mean. If you'd stop talking in riddles and—" She stopped short as his meaning suddenly became clear. "Good Lord, you can't mean *that*!"

"What?"

"That we should consummate the marriage!"

"Of course not," he replied gruffly. "Good Lord, it never even crossed my mind."

"Of course not. Forgive me. I'm afraid I misunderstood."

"Martha, I assure you, nothing is going to happen upstairs. Relax. All I was trying to say was that even if we did get carried away with our acting, it wouldn't be the end of the world. Why, we could legitimately go upstairs right now and consummate our marriage and who would care? We're adults. We answer to no one but ourselves."

"But we won't get carried away," she said quickly.

"Of course not," he agreed just as quickly. "We wouldn't think of it. Forget I even said anything."

"As if I could."

"Why? Would it be so horrible? Do you find the thought of sleeping with me that repugnant?"

"Of course not, Jake. It's just that we agreed before we even came here that we wouldn't. If we did slip, think about how it would complicate things. I'm your secretary, after all. And even worse, we wouldn't be able to annul our marriage. We'd have to go through a divorce."

"Leave it to my ever-practical secretary to remind me to keep both feet firmly planted on the ground and both hands on my own side of the bed."

"I wish you wouldn't joke about this, Jake. We have a lot at stake here. Let's not complicate matters unnecessarily."

"I wouldn't dream of it."

"Good," she said, "because I'm not really interested in an island dalliance. When I agreed to doing this, I told you I wouldn't make love with you and I meant it. Don't go thinking you'll change my mind, because you won't. I don't want to get involved in that way. Is that clear?"

"It's clear you think that's what you want."

"Whatever do you mean by that?"

He shrugged. "Don't forget, I kissed you quite a bit to-day. Those kisses spoke volumes, sweetheart."

"Meaning?"

Jake grinned. "Honey, if ever a woman wanted more than a platonic relationship, it's you."

"That's utterly absurd!" she cried. "I don't know what you're talking about. Just because you've had some success with *other* women, Jake, don't think you'll have it with *me*!'' With that, she rose from the table and stalked out of the dining room.

"Of all the lowdown, conniving, *rotten* things," Martha grumbled, slamming a drawer and catching her diaphanous nightgown in it. "Damn!" She opened the drawer and released the soft folds of the gown, then stood staring at it in dismay. She'd listened to Laurie and bought only the sheerest, sexiest underwear and nightgowns. She didn't have a serviceable, practical piece of clothing with her, outside of the Bermuda shorts and shirt she'd worn earlier.

She stared down at the sheer black nylon gown with its lace-covered décolletage. How could she wear this now, after what had transpired between her and Jake? She wished she had a pair of Dr. Dentons—something she could button up from head to foot to keep Jake's marauding hands at bay.

Sighing, she realized she was truly in for it. She was stuck in the same room with an extraordinarily appealing man for the next three weeks, with only the sheerest, sexiest clothing to hold him off. She laughed ironically to herself and sank onto the bed. What a mess! And she had walked into it with her eyes wide open, refusing to face the fact that it was an impossible situation.

Well, she was facing it now, and she was determined to keep Jake at arm's length. Something about the gleam in his eyes set her teeth on edge. She was damned if she would ever let him know she found him attractive. She had her pride, after all. She wasn't some young chick he could just waggle his finger at and seduce into his bed.

She would stymie him at every turn. She would erect barriers so high he'd never scale them. She would fight him off, and three weeks from now, she'd leave St. Matthew's with her head held high. No egotistical jackass was going to bring her down—not without one hell of a fight.

Then she sank back on the bed and stared up at the ceiling, remembering how it had felt when Jake had kissed her on the beach. She'd liked the feel of his strong arms and shoulders, had gloried in his weight pressing her into the sand. Something in her had risen as if to greet him, had wanted more even as she protested she didn't. No, she had to admit it—she wasn't fighting just Jake Molloy, she was fighting herself.

So be it. She would fight her own desires and she would win the battle. She got up and put the gown back in the drawer. She was damned if she'd sleep in that thing tonight. It would be like adding kerosene to a fire. Her eyes fell on Jake's white shirt, which lay discarded on a chair. Slowly she began to smile. Of course, it was prefect. He would never find her attractive in his own shirt. She'd look like a lanky teenager. She wasn't voluptuous, after all, and wouldn't be hiding any ripe curves beneath the fabric. It would be like being back in the office, cloaked beneath her baggy clothes.

Satisfied that she'd stumbled on the perfect defense, she hurried into the bathroom and quickly prepared for bed. She wanted to be under the covers and asleep—or pretending to be—when Jake returned. She piled her hair on top of her head and pinned it haphazardly, hoping to look as unappealing as possible. Dragging on the shirt, she rushed around gathering up her clothes at the same time she tried to brush her teeth.

Having finished in the bathroom, she raced into the bedroom and pushed her clothing into the bottom of the closet, then hurried to the bed and turned back the sheets. Just as she heard Jake's key in the lock, she realized she hadn't buttoned his shirt. Suppressing a shriek, she got two buttons fastened in the middle of the shirt, and then her hair began to fall loose. At that moment, as she stood nearly naked by the bed, her hair tumbling gloriously from its confines, Jake opened the door and walked in.

She stared at him, her arms raised to fix her hair, his enormous shirt open halfway down her chest. The shirttails flapped around her slender legs, and because her arms were lifted, the bottom of the shirt opened, revealing a hint of shadow at the top of her thighs.

Jake's gaze wandered down her body, taking in every detail, then sliding up again to come to rest on her face.

"I thought you'd be in bed already," he said.

"I'd hoped I would be."

Jake hesitated. "I want to apologize for what I said earlier."

"Oh?"

He rubbed a large hand over his jaw. "Yes, I'm sorry it ever happened. It was the champagne. I had too much of it, I'm afraid. It took a walk on the beach to sober me up and make me realize what I'd said. I can assure you, Martha, I won't lay a hand on you tonight, or any other night, for that matter. I'll abide strictly by my word. We'll have to continue to play the happily married couple in public, but when we're in our room, we'll act as if there's nothing between us."

"There isn't," she agreed reasonably.

"That's right, there isn't."

Somehow the words seemed phony. Martha looked away from Jake, unable to meet his eyes. "Well, if you don't mind, I'm going to turn off my light. I'm rather tired after all that's happened today."

"Of course. Would it bother you if I sat up and read awhile?"

"Not at all. I'll be asleep the moment my head hits the pillow."

How proficient she was becoming at lying, she thought as she slipped into bed and turned off her light. She was wide-awake. The thought of drifting off to sleep as if nothing were wrong was preposterous. How could she sleep when Jake Molloy was unbuttoning his shirt? She stared at him through her lashes while trying to pretend she was asleep. Her mouth went dry and her heartbeat quickened. He was beautiful. He was in perfect shape, with not an excess pound in sight. Her palms itched to touch him, to feel the powerful muscles that coiled just under his silken skin. When he unzipped his trousers and took them off, she had to suppress a moan. He flung them over a chair, then picked up a paper and got into bed.

She held her breath, afraid to move. He settled beneath the cover, propped two pillows beneath his head, snapped on his bedside light and began to rattle the papers.

That did it. It was bad enough she had to pretend she didn't find Jake attractive. Now she also had to put up with his noise.

"Jake," she said carefully, her eyes still shut, "must you make so much noise?"

"I'm sorry," he apologized innocently. "Am I bothering you?"

She opened one eyes and glared at him. "I can't sleep. You sound like a cat in a bag."

"I thought you were going to be asleep by the time your head hit the pillow."

She sighed and turned on her back. "It's no use. This whole situation is impossible. I can't sleep with you, Jake. It just won't work."

"Sure, it will. You're just a little nervous. It's obvious you're not the kind of woman who can fall into bed with just any man, so this is probably very unnerving. Turn over, sweetheart, and I'll shut off my light. You'll be asleep in no time."

She turned over. True to his word, Jake turned out the light, but she didn't fall asleep. Wide-awake, she lay and stared at the shadows that danced on the window shutters. Far away, music played softly, punctuated by the muted sound of laughter. Outside, the tree frogs kept up the unceasing chorus.

Soon Jake's breathing evened out and she realized he was asleep. Turning over carefully, she stared at him. Until today, she'd never been in such an intimate position with him. She felt an urge to cuddle up to him and let his solid bulk comfort her, but she knew that might wake him, and how would she explain herself? Sighing, she closed her eyes and tried to clear her mind, but it was no use. Finally she stretched out her hand until it came in contact with his skin. Smiling, she allowed herself the pleasure of stroking his arm. In his sleep, he turned toward her and flung an arm over her side. She lay very still, then tried to inch out from beneath him. It was no use; she was stuck.

But, oh, what a glorious prison. She felt her body grow warm and pliable, felt warmth shimmering inside her, heating her blood and making her tremble with awareness of both him and herself. She closed her eyes and dreamed about making love with him. As her fantasies grew more vivid, she felt her body become more and more aroused. How she wanted Jake! She wanted to stroke his skin and touch him intimately, wanted more than anything for him to wake up and not listen to her sensible pleas to stay uninvolved. She wished he would simply take matters in his own strong hands and make love to her.

Taking an unsteady breath, she inched closer to him and rested her head against his powerful chest, then listened in enchantment to the steady thud of his heart. Slowly, hesitantly, making sure she wouldn't wake him, she moved her hand down his body, growing more and more aroused by the moment.

He was magnificent. She loved the feel of his strong muscles, the silkiness of his skin, the feathery tickle of the hair that grew on his chest, arms and legs. She inched even closer and pressed the entire length of her body along his, glorying in the feel of him, the heat of his body against hers. She would move away in a moment, she promised herself, finally closing her eyes and allowing herself to enjoy his presence. She would move away before she fell asleep. She would. She really would....

She awoke, fully aroused, to the feel of Jake's hand wandering over her naked body. Gasping softly, she wondered if he were awake, then realized he was slowly waking up but wasn't fully conscious yet. When he moved his hand over her breast and began rubbing her already rigid nipple, she thought she would moan out load.

"Jake," she whispered shakily. "Jake, please..."

"Shh," he murmured, and moved his body on top of hers and began to kiss her nipples.

She groaned then, but she couldn't keep her hands from moving up and down his broad back, couldn't keep him from touching her, arousing her, driving her mad with desire. His manhood was insistent, pressing into her abdomen while his strong leg thrust itself between hers. At first she tried to stop him, but she couldn't fight it. Her body wanted what he wanted. She opened her legs and he slid between them.

She went rigid at the feel of his arousal nudging against her, then the rigidity left and she found herself breathing heavily, arching her back so her breasts were crushed against the rock-hard wall of his chest. She was on fire; the pulsing between her legs was driving her mad. She panted breathlessly and clung to Jake as he sucked first one nipple, then the other. His hands moved incessantly over her body, urging her to respond. She couldn't resist; didn't want to. All the desire in the world centered itself within her vibrating womanhood, urging fulfillment. She needed it; was mad for it; would die if she didn't get it—

A loud knock on the door made them freeze. Jake rose up on his elbows and stared down into her face. She stared back.

"Dammit," he explained. "I asked room service to bring us our breakfast at eight."

She didn't say a word.

"I could tell them to leave," he said at last.

She closed her eyes and pushed him off her. "No, we . . . We were asleep. We didn't know what we were doing. Tell them to come in."

Muttering a curse, Jake rolled over and yelled for the maid to come in. Martha pulled the covers up to her neck. Beneath the sheets, she struggled to button Jake's shirt.

"Good morning," greeted the maid, smiling at them as she set a tray over Jake's lap, then another over Martha's. "It is a beautiful day. The sun he shines in the blue sky, the birds sing, the ocean visits St. Matthew's Island. You will love today. You will find out this is truly paradise."

"Yeah," Jake replied sullenly. "Great."

Martha hit his arm beneath the covers and flashed a wide smile at the young woman. "I'm sure we're going to love it here."

"You surprise us in the kitchen," the maid said, chattering as she walked around opening the shutters to admit the sun. "Most honeymooners, they never even come out of their room for a day or two. Breakfast at eight, though—we all laugh and wonder if you sane!"

"Oh, we're sane all right," Jake groused, shoving a piece of toast into his mouth. "We're sane as can be."

"Jake," Martha warned under her breath.

"You want anything else?" the maid asked, smiling broadly from the door.

"Not a thing," Jake answered. "Just leave us in peace."

"Jake!" Martha cried out, shocked at his behavior.

"Okay!" the young woman said gaily. "See you! Have a nice day." She giggled behind her hand. "I think you have a *very* nice day, no?"

"No," Jake muttered. Then the maid was gone and he turned to Martha. "All right, sweetheart, we're going to have this thing out."

Seven

There is nothing, as you put it, to have out," Martha said. "What happened just now was a mistake."

"A mistake?" Jake crowed. "My God, woman, we were making love and it felt good, and you call it a *mistake*?"

"We were not making love," she snapped. She was stuck in the bed, laden down by a full breakfast tray while Jake stood over her, his hands on his hips. She'd never felt so trapped in her life.

"What would you call it, then?" he asked. "Shaking hands?"

"Technically, it would qualify as foreplay, I suppose," she answered primly. "But that doesn't mean it should ever have happened."

"That doesn't mean it should ever have happened," Jake mimicked. He let out a frustrated sigh. "All right, have it your way. I just don't see anything wrong with taking advantage of the situation we're in and enjoying ourselves."

"Well, I do."

"Obviously." His eyes danced with amusement. "But sweetheart, would you do me a favor tonight?"

She lifted her gaze. "What would you like?"

"Don't wear any more of my shirts to bed, okay? Nothing turns me on more than the sight of a woman wearing a man's shirt."

Mortified, she felt her face turn bright red. "I . . . I didn't know. All I have with me are those silly lace and silk negligees, and I was afraid they'd . . . um . . ."

"So you were deliberately trying to make yourself unappealing, eh? Too bad it didn't work." He walked over to the side of the bed and rested his fists on either side of her. "You know, Martha Molloy, this trip is turning out to be truly fascinating. For five years I've worked with you and I never knew you were attractive. But suddenly my hands are just itching to touch you. I want to feel your breasts in my palms. I want to suck your nipples and drive you mad with passion." He reached out and lightly brushed her cheek with his knuckles. "What do you think of that?"

She couldn't take her eyes off him. She was mesmerized, trapped in his gaze like a deer caught in a hunter's sights. "I . . . I . . ." She moistened her lips with her tongue, then regretted the action. Jake's eyes were fastened on her mouth. She felt a spasm of awareness flash through her, turning her body to musky heat. "I think you'd better go," she finally managed.

"I think you're right," he said, leaning over her to drop a soft kiss on her lips. "This could get to be dangerous, couldn't it?" he whispered.

She took a steadying breath, keeping her eyes closed so she couldn't see him. It felt safer that way. "What are we going to do today? About investigating the hotel, I mean," she added quickly.

"If you'd open your eyes and look at me, I'd tell you."

Reluctantly she opened her eyes. Jake was seated on the edge of the bed, a small smile playing about his mouth. "I thought we'd rent a jeep and take a ride around the island. We could have the kitchen prepare us a picnic lunch. It would give us a chance to reconnoiter. I'd like you to see the site for our hotel. It's rather remote, though, so you'd better dress in jeans.''

"But aren't you afraid Bert will see us?''

"We'll just be two honeymooners who stumbled on a remote track that led to the new hotel site. I'll wear a bushman's hat and sunglasses. He won't recognize me. If he knew I was on the island it would be different, but he doesn't, and he's never even seen you. No, I think we'll be pretty safe. Anyway, I don't plan on actually approaching the workers. I just want you to see the site, and I'd like to take a look around on the sly. Maybe we'll see something going on that looks out of the ordinary.''

"And if we do?''

Jake shrugged. "We'll file it away in our memory banks and get on with the investigation elsewhere.''

"But aren't there security guards?'' she asked doubtfully.

"Sure, but they're only on duty at night.'' Jake laughed. "Sweetie, you forget, we're going to look like honeymooners. Any workers worth their salt will know what we've got our minds on, and it ain't gonna be hotels.''

She lifted her chin. "It sounds to me like a ruse, all right, but I'm wondering what your real aim is—to find out about the hotel, or to have your way with me.''

"Maybe it's a little bit of both.''

She tilted her head, fixing Jake with determined blue eyes. "Forget it, Jake. I'm here to help you find out what's holding up construction on the hotel, and that's all I'm here for.''

"You are the embodiment of the Puritan ethic,'' he said, shaking his head sorrowfully. "Such a shame. We could be having a wonderful time together, taking advantage of this fortuitous circumstance.''

"Let's just concentrate on the investigation, shall we?" she suggested sweetly, "and leave the enjoyment for some other time."

"There's no time like the present, sweetheart."

She sat back against the pillows. "You know, this is really a surprise. After working for you all this time, I'm only just now realizing you're a rake."

He laughed delightedly. "You may want to call me a rake, but the truth is, I'm just a red-blooded man who woke up this morning next to a willing female. I simply did what came naturally." His gray eyes laughed into hers. "And so did you—if you'd only admit it."

"I admit nothing of the sort," she retorted, pushing the breakfast tray away and preparing to get up. "Now, if you'll excuse me, I have to get dressed."

"Fine," he said. "Go ahead."

She turned in amazement. "You mean you're just going to sit there and *watch*?"

Jake picked up a piece of cold toast and began munching on it contentedly. "Why not? We're married, aren't we? It would look awful funny if I continue to leave the room every time you need to shower or dress."

"But—" She stared at him, unable to find words to describe her disbelief. "Jake, this is ridiculous. I refuse to let you do this. At least have the courtesy to go into the bathroom while I dress."

"My dear, if you need the privacy so badly, go into the bathroom yourself and get dressed there."

"All right, I will!" she declared, hopping out of bed. She thought she would make a clean getaway, but to her dismay, found herself trapped. Her shirttails were caught beneath one of Jake's legs. She tugged at them, but he refused to budge. "Will you please move!" she snapped.

"No," he said agreeably. "I have a better idea. Why don't you join me here? We could lie on the bed in the sunshine and get to know each other a little better."

She put her hands on her hips, gazing down at him knowingly. "You are incorrigible."

"Yes, I am at that," he agreed, grinning. He pushed the breakfast tray away and lay back, patting the mattress next to him. "Come on, Martha, be a sport. Stop being such a priss and have a little fun."

"I'm not here to have fun," she snapped, "and neither are you." But even as she turned away, she saw him reach out and grasp her arm.

"I think you *are* here to have fun," he said slowly. "I think that's precisely what you want. You're just afraid to admit it."

"I'm not afraid of anything."

"Prove it."

Her eyes met Jake's. She was about to shake his hand off her arm, but the next thing she knew, he'd pulled her onto the bed. Suddenly she was on her back and Jake was leaning over her, with one strong leg thrown over hers.

"I think it's time we did a little more acting, don't you?" he murmured.

She lay looking up at him, feeling the small circle of heat that drummed in her midsection slowly expand. The desire she'd kept at bay since waking up overpowered her. When she didn't push him away, he took her lack of resistance for compliance. Slowly he began to unbutton her shirt until she lay naked beneath him. Gently he stroked his hand over her body, gradually approaching her breasts but moving away before he touched them. Her breathing grew heavy. She told herself to push Jake away, but his teasing touch kept her from doing it.

He sent her over the edge when he slid his hand beneath her legs. She moaned softly, then pulled his head down and kissed him. She clung to him, giving herself up to the sweetness of his kisses.

Her trembling betrayed her. Jake gathered her in his strong arms and covered her with kisses. She lay beneath him, drowning in ecstasy, her eyes closed as she drank in his lovemaking. Slowly he moved his hand, cupping her womanhood and beginning a slow, erotic massage.

She went rigid for a moment, then let out a low sob. He continued massaging her and she went rigid again, trying to hold off the golden ripples that threatened to overpower her.

"Oh, Jake," she whispered. "I don't think we should be doing this."

"Yes," he murmured. "I think we should."

She gasped at the shock of the first wave, then lost herself in fluid energy, crying out when the ripples tore through her body and sent her spinning into space. He moved his hand up and cupped her breast, lowering his lips to her swollen nipple and slowly sucking it into his mouth. His tongue swirled around it, washing it in erotic juices. She held his head to her breast, still gasping from the shock of her climax. But though she expected the need to dissolve, it didn't. Under Jake's expert lovemaking, her need grew again, mushrooming out of control until she lay beneath him, trembling with such desire that she couldn't articulate her needs, could do nothing but lie back and drown in the stunning pleasure that cascaded over her.

Only the shrill ringing of the phone stopped them from making love. Jake muttered a low curse and lay back, staring into her eyes as the phone continued to ring incessantly.

"I suppose we'd better answer it," he said.

"I suppose so."

Sighing, he rose up on one elbow and grabbed the phone. The sudden silence was startling. Martha lay beside him, listening as he spoke into the phone.

"Yes," he replied. "No, no bother."

Martha smiled, amused at his obvious lie.

"Mmm-hmm, I see. No, no, that's quite all right. Yes, we'll be happy to. Of course not. Yes. Yes, of course."

He hung up and lay back down, letting out a sigh as he scratched his bare chest. "Well, I'll be damned."

"What is it?" she asked.

He put an arm under his head to serve as a pillow. "That was the desk. It seems a tropical storm is approaching the island. They wanted to warn us in case we had plans to go out today."

"Oh." Martha turned her head to look at Jake. "We were going to have a picnic. Can't we go now?"

"I was growing quite comfortable here, but I suppose we could still go. The desk clerk said the storm wouldn't be arriving for about ten to twelve hours, but he just wanted us to know. They're warning all the guests. He asked us to tell them where we'll be going if we do go out. They're concerned for their guests' safety and all that."

"I see." Martha looked away, quickly beginning to button Jake's shirt. Her fingers shook and she was unable to meet his eyes. She couldn't help but remember what had just transpired between them. Somehow she had to defuse the situation, lest Jake think she wanted more of the same.

"I think I did a pretty good acting job just now, don't you?" she remarked breezily.

"*Acting?*" Jake began to chuckle. "If you insist that's what it was, I'll go along with you, but I've been with women who tried to pretend. I know the difference."

"Do you?" she asked wryly, sliding off the bed and turning her back to Jake. "Well, hooray for Jake Molloy. How does it feel to know you're this macho stud who brings women such incredible pleasure?"

"It feels great," he replied, grinning at her as he rubbed his chest.

She turned her head to look at him over her shoulder. "You egotistical male," she said softly. "You really think you're something, don't you?"

"No, I really think you're something."

She gazed into his eyes a moment, then turned away, troubled by his words. Had Jake meant what he said, or was it just a line? "I'm going to shower and dress in the bath-room," she announced.

"Mmm," he murmured dreamily. "Can I come in and watch?"

She smiled despite herself. "No, you can not. Honestly, Jake, you're incredibly boring when you go on like this."

"And you love it."

"I do not!"

"Oh, yes, you do. Look at yourself when you get into the bathroom. You look like a Christmas tree, all lit up and sparkling to beat the band. Your eyes are shining, your en-tire face is filled with light. If you don't look like a woman who just enjoyed herself mightily, then my name's not Jake Molloy."

"Poo-poo," she answered mockingly, making a face at him before ducking into the bathroom. She peeked at him from behind the door. "Just stay where you are, buster. I don't feel like fighting off a lecher."

"There she goes again," he teased. "Another lie, all be-cause she feels she has to save face."

"I do not!" she protested.

"Do, too."

She hesitated a moment, considering hitting him with a pillow, then she settled for slamming the door. Somehow that felt incredibly good—almost as good as being in bed with him.

An hour later, they'd packed a picnic lunch in a jeep and were ready to set off to explore the island.

"Don't go too far," Sidney Howell warned them. "We don't get many storms on St. Matthew's, but what few we get are extraordinary."

"We'll remember that," Jake replied. "But don't worry if we're not back right away. We'll find shelter if we have to."

Sidney looked past Jake to Martha. His eyes seemed to communicate worry, but she couldn't be sure. She wasn't used to being taken care of by men. Proud, self-sufficient Martha was her own caretaker. Yet she had to admit she felt a thrill of excitement when Jake looked from Sidney to her and his mouth tightened into a grim line of disapproval. He started the jeep with an extra loud revving of the engine and put it into gear. They took off like a jackrabbit, with gravel spraying the road beneath their tires.

"Maybe we should have postponed our trip," Martha suggested, eyeing the blue skies overhead. There didn't seem to be any sign of a storm in the vicinity, but perhaps they came on quickly.

"Are you worried?" Jake asked, casting her a quick look.

"Not really, but Sidney Howell sure seemed to be."

"Sidney Howell, my dear, is worried about you—not the storm."

"Why would he worry about me?"

"Because he's obviously smitten. I don't think he likes the idea of your being married. He's jealous."

"Oh, come *on*, Jake!"

"You don't believe me? When we get back tonight, spend a little time alone with him. See for yourself. I'll bet you a hundred bucks he comes on to you."

"That's ridiculous!"

"Martha, so far I can discover only one thing wrong with you—you're completely untutored in the ways of the opposite sex. Fortunately, I find this particular quirk of yours endearing. I might not, though, if you let our friend Sidney take advantage of you."

"Jake," she answered wryly, "I don't even let *you* take advantage of me, much less a stranger like Sidney Howell."

"Just be sure you keep it that way, sweetheart," he replied, throwing her an amused look. "I don't mind scaling your defenses, but I don't want Howell to get any ideas. Just remember you're a married woman, and you're married to a fiercely possessive man."

"Until three weeks from now, when this whole thing will be over and we'll be back in New York, trying to get our quickie marriage annulled. How will we explain it to the judge, Jake? That we had a momentary passion that never quite panned out when we got married?"

"Let's not worry about that now. Just sit back and enjoy the ride. What did I tell you about St. Matthew's being the most beautiful spot on earth?"

"You were right," she conceded, breathing in the scents of hibiscus and fragrant frangipani. Masses of lavender and purple bougainvillea lined the narrow dirt road, turning the jungle into a tropical garden. Agapanthus lilies formed a blue carpet on the sides of the road, vying with lavender hydrangeas and pink azalea bushes for their vibrant color.

Occasionally they would happen upon a small pocket of civilization where cats and dogs lazed on front porches, goats wandered untethered on the roads, and skimpily dressed children dashed out to wave as they passed by. Small white stucco huts with red-tiled roofs dotted the hillsides, which were almost hidden from view by the dense vegetation.

They passed numerous small waterfalls where the music of the water competed with the chatter of green parrots and yellow-feathered bananaquits. Deep within the forested regions, peahens honked for their mates. Once a hermit crab, obviously lost, ambled across the road after they'd stopped to let it pass.

They drove for over an hour, inching their way slowly over the deeply rutted dirt roads. This was no place for slapdash, headlong speed. It was truly a paradise, utterly different from Martha and Jake's usual world of grid-locked traffic, honking horns and rushing pedestrians.

Martha smiled as she remembered driving with her parents as a child. "When I was a little girl," she said to Jake, "my parents would take me out riding in the car. I can remember sitting in the back seat and hating every minute of it. There always came the time when I'd get tired, so I'd say, 'Are we there yet?'" She laughed delightedly. "My parents always scolded me and told me to be quiet. I think that's when I began to enjoy rebelling so much."

Jake glanced at her, a smile on his face. "And I suppose that story's a hint to tell you if we're there yet."

She laughed, throwing her head back in sheer pleasure as the island breeze combed her hair with hits silken fingers. "You're catching on to my indirect questions rather quickly, Jake. Yes, as a matter of fact, I do want to know how far we have to go."

"Not far," he told her. "It's a small island. Even crawling like this we'll be there in a few minutes. I'll find a place to park off to the side of the road. We can take our lunch and wander toward the construction. If anyone questions us, we'll say we were merely looking for a good place to have a picnic."

"If I'd known you were into espionage, I might not have taken the job five years ago when you offered it to me."

"But think what you'd be missing." Jake pulled the jeep to a stop by the side of the road. "Look." He pointed left, toward a magnificent, unspoiled beach that stretched as far as the eye could see. Gentle waves washed ashore, spilling over the sand like white lace, then returning to the sea, dragging shells and small water-smoothed stones back with them."

"It's perfect," Martha declared wonderingly. "Absolutely perfect."

"And up there," Jake said, pointing upward to the right, "that's where the Hilliard will be."

Martha felt a strange thrill go through her. For over a year, Jake had talked about St. Matthew's, location of the next Hilliard Hotel. She had typed his letters, taken his correspondence and shuttled phone calls back and forth, but this was her first sight of the magnificent place itself.

"It will be truly beautiful," she said in awe, taking in the native flowering shrubs that clung to the rising slopes. Off to one side, a magnificent mist-shrouded waterfall tumbled over mossy rocks. Bordered by dense green ferns and other tropical foliage, the waterfall seemed to have been carved out of the hillside. Fog layered the top of the hill where the hotel would someday sit. There was something primeval about the setting, as if it hadn't yet been discovered by man.

Martha shivered unexpectedly, feeling an odd premonition. Perhaps this magnificent place shouldn't be disturbed. Maybe Hilliard was wrong to build here and destroy the stupendous natural beauty. In its cloak of mist and fog, this spot seemed to beg for mercy, silently asking to remain untouched by human hands.

Suddenly Martha felt an urgent need to touch Jake, to anchor herself in his solidity. Reaching out, she put her hand in his. "It's so beautiful," she murmured. "I'm almost sorry this is the spot you've chosen."

"Sorry?" He looked at her in disbelief, then began to laugh. "My God, Martha, have you been the one behind the work stoppages all along?"

She smiled, but her smile quickly faded as she surveyed the majestic mountain. "Look at it, Jake. It's magnificent." She frowned, remembering other places that had struck her this way. "It's like the redwoods in California, or New Hampshire's Cathedral in the Pines. Sometimes there are special places on this earth that should never be touched."

"You don't know me very well, do you, Martha?" Jake said quietly.

Startled, she turned to look at him. "What do you mean?"

"Simply that I would never allow this place to be destroyed. It *is* a special spot, and I worked very closely with the architect to ensure that it wouldn't be turned into a tourist trap.'' He pointed toward the hill. ''Perhaps you've forgotten all those letters you typed, but I'll remind you now of the special pains we're taking with this site. We're not putting a road through just yet. We're merely thinning the vegetation so the workers can carry the construction materials up the hill. Instead of building our usual high rise, we've opted to build separate cabanas that nestle into the hillside. They'll be connected to the main building and each other by wooden walkways.''

''Yes,'' she replied slowly. ''I remember all that, but somehow...'' She frowned again, puzzled by the strong reaction she was having. ''It's just a feeling I get, as if the place itself doesn't want to be disturbed....''

''I can assure you, Mrs. Molloy, that this place, magnificent as it may be, doesn't give two figs about what's done to it. Now, shall we get out and hike up to the top?''

Putting on a smile, she nodded her head in agreement. ''Yes, let's do that.''

She told herself she'd only been imagining things. Jake was right: trees and waterfalls and flowering shrubs didn't care what happened to them. Only people cared.

Thoughtfully she looked even more closely at her surroundings. If they found out who cared the most about this mountaintop, she had a hunch they would find out who was behind the work stoppages at the Hilliard Hotel.

Eight

—

A green parrot flew out of the thick foliage above them, squawking its protest at their arrival in its splendid home. To the right, water crashed over the steep falls, sending mist high into the air and forming a rainbow overhead. Bougainvillea and azalea grew in masses along the way, competing with orchids and other exotic plants for their attention. Everything seemed like a fantasy—surely only Walt Disney could have created this. Martha half expected to see Tarzan—clad only in a loincloth—emerge from the dense green depths, his shouted call competing with the cheerful chatter of chimpanzees.

But there were no ape-men here, no chimpanzees, no Hollywood directors shouting instructions through megaphones. This mountain was real—a marvelous, untouched wonderland cloaked in fog and shrouded in mist, standing like a monolith in testament to the beauty of nature.

They were halfway up the hillside when Jake put a hand on Martha's arm and motioned for her to be quiet.

"What is it?" she whispered.

He shook his head. "I thought I heard something."

They stood motionless, listening to the sounds of the tropical jungle. Birds chattered, leaves rustled in the breeze, water rushed over the waterfall, rumbling in the background like the sound of troops marching in the distance.

Finally Jake smiled at Martha. "I guess I'm hearing things."

"Shall I bring you back to the hotel and lock you up?"

He grinned. "Only if you stay with me."

"Jake Molloy, how you go on. I swear you'd charm the knickers off my ninety-two-year-old grandmother."

"If your grandmother were like you, she'd charm the knickers off *me*."

Martha considered Jake. Was he really such a charming rogue, given to glib lies and easy lines? Or could he mean all this bunk he was spouting?

"You're transparent, my dear," Jake remarked, taking her hand and leading her up the overgrown path.

"Oh? In what way?"

"I can see you studying me, trying to figure out why I'm saying these wild and unbelievable things about you."

"Why are you?"

"Because they're true."

"Oh? Then why haven't you been chasing me around the office these past five years? Do your hormones only start working in the tropics?"

Jake chuckled. "My hormones work just fine, here or in New York. But that's an interesting question. I've been giving it a lot of thought, myself."

"And what have you come up with?"

Jake stopped and turned to Martha, his eyes narrowed as he studied her. "I think it's Bloomingdale's," he said at last, nodding his head judiciously.

"Bloomingdale's!"

"That makeover job they did on you," he explained, motioning inarticulately with one hand. "You know—the haircut, the makeup, the new clothes. They've changed you overnight into this rather attractive woman whom I find enormously appealing."

Martha snorted—rather unattractively, she thought—and turned away, charging ahead up the path, trying to keep her heartbeat steady, telling herself not to be so absurdly pleased with the malarkey Jake was spouting.

Chuckling, he came after her, grabbing her hand and spinning her around to face him. "Ah ha!" he said, grinning at her. "She blushes! The comely maiden hides behind a modest façade, pretending not to like the gentleman's advances, when all along her heartbeat quickens, the blood rushes to her cheeks, sends small signals to her overwrought brain, telling her to let down her defenses, go into his strong arms, sink into the grasses and make mad passionate love with him."

"Horse pooey," she said. "All the maiden feels is an overwhelming desire to be sick."

He shook his head disapprovingly. "No, no, no, Martha. You've got to drop the sardonic, acidic tone and be more yielding. You've got to bat those lashes of yours and simper a bit."

"*Simper?* Over my dead body!"

Laughing, Jake reached out and drew her into his arms. "All right then, just pucker up."

She couldn't help herself—he was so absurd she had to laugh. "You foolish man," she said, laughing up at him. "Will you stop this comedy and get serious for once? We're here for very important corporate business, not to indulge ourselves in silly mooning over unattractive members of the opposite sex."

"Ah, since neither of us is unattractive, what we're doing is okay."

"What?" she asked, still laughing. "Who says you're so attractive, Jake Molloy? You've got this jaw that's chipped from granite and a nose only a prizefighter could love and—"

"Hush, Martha," he murmured, drawing her even closer. "Stop fighting me."

His quiet words sent their playful mood packing. Suddenly she was standing in his arms, looking up into his gray eyes, overwhelmed by new feelings that clamored for expression.

"That's right," he insisted. "Kiss me. Give in to it, Martha. It's inevitable."

"But I don't—"

He stopped her with a searing kiss that sent her reeling. She clung to him to keep from losing her balance, digging her fingers into his shoulders even as she tried to break free. As her resistance melted, the kiss changed, becoming more gentle even as it deepened. Slowly she wound her arms around his neck. Sweetness such as she had never experienced overwhelmed her, moving through her body on a supercharged tide of heat.

Bending her gently back, Jake let his lips explore the creamy curve of her shoulder, then lowered them to the shadowy crevice between her breasts. Breathless, she closed her eyes in rapture, clinging to him, all resistance gone, replaced by feelings that trembled inside her.

Wonderingly she moved her hand over his face, gently exploring the smoothly shaven skin, lightly touching his dark brows and thick hair, then running her fingers along his jawline. He took her hand and thrust it inside his shirt. She gasped slightly and ran her hand over his chest, enjoying the feel of the dark hairs that covered it even as she noted the firm muscles that rippled down to his belt buckle.

Slowly he pulled his shirt from his trousers and began unbuttoning it, all the while holding her with one arm so she couldn't escape the musky scent of his body. She closed her eyes and let him lower her to the ground. After he'd shaken off the pack he carried, he took her hand and placed it over his heart.

"You see?" he whispered. "This is because of you."

Lying on her back, she lifted confused eyes to his. "I don't understand what's happening."

"Don't try to. Just enjoy it."

"But Jake—"

He shook his head and placed a finger lightly against her lips. "Shh," he warned. "Maybe some things should not be analyzed. Maybe some things are just meant to be."

She closed her eyes, trying to shut out the sight of him. But she couldn't shut out his scent, or the feel of him, or the sound of his low voice whispering against her throat as he kissed her.

"Touch me," he murmured. "I love your hands on my skin."

She was helpless to resist. Everything in her rose up in compliance. She gave a small, inarticulate moan and put her arms around him, moving her hands over his back, glorying in the way the muscles rippled under his silken skin. Pleasure cascaded over her, warming her response. She kissed him hungrily, moving her hands over his back and shoulders, urging him closer, gasping softly as he unbuttoned her blouse and thrust his hand inside her bra.

He moved his thumb back and forth over her nipple, making it harden in response. Slowly he reached behind her and unfastened her bra. She felt it fall away, releasing her from its bonds to those of pleasure.

"Oh, Jake," she whispered, moving her hand over his cheek. "It feels so good when you touch me. I wish it could go on like this forever."

"It can," he murmured, lowering his head to nuzzle her breast with his lips and tongue. "It will."

She heard his words and tried to hold on to the precious mood that had enveloped them, but some small demon

wouldn't be ignored. "It will for the next few weeks, anyway," she said wryly. Pushing him away, she sat up and
fastened her bra. "Not forever—as you would have me believe when you're working your magic on me." She folded
her arms and stared down at him. "Get up, Jake. We've got
spying to do."

"Hell's bells, you're efficient even after making love.
Does nothing faze you, Martha?"

"Not hail nor sleet nor snow," she answered ironically.
"And once again, I have to remark that we were not making love."

"Okay, okay," he agreed disgustedly. "I know—that was
only *foreplay*."

She inclined her head, a small smile hovering on her lips.
"Quite right. I'm glad you're learning the difference."

Jake paused in buttoning his shirt and looked up at her,
his face grave as he studied her. "You know, Martha, I'll let
you get away with that now, but someday I'm going to teach
you that I know very well the difference between foreplay
and making love."

She suppressed a small shiver and turned away, not
wanting him to see the effect his words had on her. Suddenly she wished that she hadn't given in to her practical
side. Who cared if their marriage would only last a matter
of weeks? As Jake had said last night, it was a legal and
valid marriage—why not enjoy it while she could?

But something held her back. Somewhere deep inside, she
felt the stirrings of something far more precious than physical fulfillment. She was besieged with extraordinary con-
flict. Her body wanted Jake, but her heart wanted him, too.
Without knowing why, she intuitively recognized that her
heart would never win him if she gave in to him too soon.
Love, at least in the early stages, was a game, after all,
and—

She came to a stop on the path, stunned at her thoughts.
Love? Was she truly falling in *love* with Jake Molloy?

Turning, she stared at him, watching as he got up and dusted off his jeans, then leaned over to pick up the backpack that contained their lunch.

"What?" Jake asked, looking up to find her staring at him.

She shook her head, telling herself she wouldn't recognize love if she fell over it. "Nothing. I just had a thought, but I realized it was ludicrous."

"Something about me?"

She smiled slowly, enjoying her private joke. "Yes. That's why it's so ludicrous."

"I'll get you yet, you know."

"Oh, will you, now? How bold of you to throw down such a challenging gauntlet."

"You know what's wrong with you, Martha?"

"The way you've been acting recently, I wasn't aware anything was."

He ignored her sarcasm and went on. "You're still acting like my employee. You haven't been able to drop the office mannerisms. You think I expect you to be cool and efficient, even when we're together like this."

"Don't you?"

"No. I'd like you to give in to that softer side of yours— the one you're so unfamiliar with it scares you silly."

She tossed her head and turned her back on Jake. "Listen to the man make a fool of himself," she said airily. "On and on he goes, analyzing something he knows nothing about."

"That's where you're wrong," he corrected, falling into step beside her. "I know a lot about women."

That gave her momentary pause. She tripped on an exposed root, then hurried on, hiding her jealousy behind indifference. "Go ahead, Jake, crank out the stories of past conquests. Turn me green with envy. Make my blood simmer." She turned cool eyes on him. "None of it will work, Molloy. I'm immune."

"To steal your phrase—horse pooey."

She couldn't continue to look into his eyes. They were too knowing, too filled with amusement at her expense. Again she tossed her head, pretending she didn't give a fig for what he thought. She was about to crash ahead into the depths of the junglelike growth when Jake reached out and took her arm, spinning her around.

"Good grief, Jake," she said, faking weariness. "Not now, for heaven's sake."

But he wasn't paying her any mind. He was staring over her shoulder, his eyes narrowed as he gazed at some distant object. He put a finger to his lips to signal her to be quiet, then pointed in the direction he was looking. Without making a sound, she turned and looked.

Her eyes widened. Up ahead, about fifty yards away, a few men were seated in a circle. Their quiet laughter and the musical sound of their voices carried through the dense vegetation. She saw the occasional flash of a colorful shirt as someone got up and poured himself coffee, and realized they were natives, probably workers on the construction site.

But why weren't they working?

"Why are they just sitting there?" she whispered.

Jake shook his head, still staring at the men, who so far hadn't noticed them. "Could be a break. Or maybe something's wrong again—another holdup, perhaps."

"Or maybe it's one of those sacrifices." A shiver went through her. Reaching out, she put her hand in Jake's. "You know, with the chicken...."

Jake grinned and pulled her into his arms, cradling her against his chest. As she clung to him, she could feel him shaking with silent laughter.

"Good Lord, Martha," he said when he was able to speak without making too much noise. "Don't tell me that frightens you!"

"Of course it frightens me!" she whispered back. "It petrifies me. Let's get out of her before they realize we're here and sacrifice *us*."

He laughed again, hugging her and rocking her back and forth until she began to feel better simply because he found her so amusing.

"Evidently you think my fears are ludicrous," she said at last, smiling in spite of herself.

"You got it."

"I take it you think the natives are friendly."

"You met Jimmy. You met our waiter and the maid. They were friendly, weren't they?"

"Yes, but they didn't know we work for Hilliard Hotels."

"You have a point there," he admitted, then laughed softly and hugged her again.

She banged his shoulder with her fist. "Stop teasing me," she pleaded, trying to keep from laughing too loudly. "They'll hear us and we'll be history."

"I can see the headlines in the papers now—Human Sacrifice On St. Matthew's Island—Honeymooners Mistaken For Chickens And Boiled In Oil."

"Oh, stop it," she retorted, hitting his arm again playfully. "And while you're being so funny, Mr. Molloy, shouldn't you be wearing that bushman's hat you spoke about this morning? And sunglasses?"

"My God, you're right." He quickly reached into his shirt pocket and took out his sunglasses and put them on, then reached for the hat he'd stuffed into the top of the pack. Settling it on his head, he looked for all the world like Indiana Jones dressed for the Australian outback.

"My handsome husband," Martha pronounced softly. "You look like a true adventurer."

"Good. Perhaps you won't be afraid now. Even if you get kidnapped, I'll rescue you."

"My hero," she said, batting her lashes.

He drew her into his arms and kissed her, and she didn't resist. She kissed him back wholeheartedly. In their present mood, she would have done anything he requested.

"Well!" he exclaimed when they parted. "Shall we stop here for our picnic?"

"Here?"

"Why not? They've seen us now. That kiss just put the seal of authenticity on our disguise as honeymooners. Why not just settle down for a sandwich and some cold beer?"

"They've seen us?"

Jake nodded, then smiled at something behind her back. Martha whirled around, then clutched at Jake. A huge black man was standing about ten feet away, his arms folded, his skin as dark as obsidian.

"Hello," Jake said pleasantly, holding up the backpack. "We were looking for a good spot for lunch." He turned and pointed downhill toward the bay. "We've never seen such a beautiful spot for a picnic."

"Not good for picnic," the man answered. "The gods be angry."

"The gods?" Martha asked faintly.

The man smiled for the first time, inclining his head toward her in the polite way the natives were known for. "Yes, ma'am. The island gods. They live here. This mountain theirs."

"Then why are you here?"

"We guard their home," the man replied. "I am Cecil Bongo, Mumbo Jumbo of St. Matthew's island."

"Mumbo *Jumbo*?"

Jake pulled Martha into the protection of his strong arm. "That's a kind of holy man," he explained softly, then raised his voice and spoke to Cecil. "We should leave, then?"

Cecil nodded gravely, pointing to the sky. "You see? The gods, they send a storm they are so angry."

"Because of *us*?" Martha asked disbelievingly.

"Yes, because of you and other white people who come to take their home from them."

"Other white people?" Jake repeated, his voice carrying only friendly curiosity.

Cecil turned and pointed up the hill. "Up there, at the top, white men dream of building castles. The gods will weep now. They wish only to be left alone in peace."

"What sort of castle?" Martha ventured hesitantly.

"Big castle," Cecil explained. "A hundred stories high, like in New York."

"You've been to New York?" Martha asked.

"Oh yes, I go as a young man, wanting to see the world." Cecil smiled, revealing a gap in his front teeth. "I see and turn around and come home. Everyone who leave St. Matthew's always come back. Is the way. We who live in paradise never leave it for long."

"But who would build a skyscraper here?" Martha questioned. "That would be terrible. It's much too lovely here for that kind of building."

Cecil Bongo nodded. "Yes, but we have seen the plans, the what you call them? The architect's drawings. The building, it reached to the sky. It so high, it could be seen on St. Thomas, perhaps. Maybe even in South America."

"Well," said Martha, raising her eyebrows, "that *is* a tall building."

"Who showed you these plans?" Jake asked.

"The man in charge," Cecil replied. "He show us and try to get us to work, but we do not. We try to keep the gods from getting angry, but see?" He pointed to the sky again. "They *very* angry now."

"Yes," Jake agreed, staring at the dark clouds that had moved in to cover the sun. "Perhaps my wife and I should go."

"You stay at hotel?"

"Yes, we're at the Paradise."

"Ah," Cecil said, smiling. "That very good hotel. Here many, many years. Mr. Thumpwhistle, he build a good hotel. Not make the gods angry."

"Mr. *Thumpwhistle*?" Martha gasped.

"You know him?" Cecil asked, grinning. "Is he back, then?"

"Why, yes," Jake answered. "We came over on the same plane. Did you say he built the Paradise?"

Cecil laughed. "That my way of speaking. He not actually *build* it himself, but he own it. He own many hotel in the islands."

"So Oliver Thumpwhistle owns the Paradise," Jake remarked thoughtfully. "I wonder why he didn't tell us. Or why Sidney Howell didn't...."

Cecil smiled. "Mr. Thumpwhistle, he modest man. He like to stay in hotel and not let guest know who he be." Cecil grinned. "How you say it in spy movie? I blow his cover, yes?"

"I'm afraid you have," Martha said, smiling warmly. "But don't worry, we won't let him know we found out."

"Good. Mr. Thumpwhistle be very angry if he find out I tell his secret."

"You've know him for a long time then?" Jake asked.

"Many, many years. He good man. He love this island as we do. He, too, believe in our gods. He know they grow angry when island changes. We respect Mr. Thumpwhistle, listen to him. He wise, as few white men are." Cecil put a hand to his mouth. "I am sorry!" he exclaimed. "I did not mean to offend you both."

"No offense taken," Jake replied, smiling. "As a matter of fact, I'm beginning to think it was very unwise of us to take a jeep and come so far when we knew a storm was coming."

"But how you know storm was coming?" Cecil demanded curiously. "You listen to gods also?"

Jake hesitated, then explained, "Perhaps we sensed your gods were growing angry."

"Jake!" Martha whispered, shocked at what he'd said. "Don't lie to Cecil!"

"I'm not lying, sweetheart. I'm merely being diplomatic."

"Oh." She considered that, then let it go. Overhead, the sky was growing darker by the second. Suddenly she wished the jeep had a top. They would be soaked by the time they arrived back at the Paradise. She tugged at Jake's arm. "I think maybe we'd better go. It's really getting dark." She turned to Cecil and smiled. "It was very nice meeting you, Mr. Bongo. If you're near the Paradise, please come visit us."

"Yes," Cecil said, beaming with happiness at the invitation. "But I do not know your names."

"Jake and Martha," Jake responded quickly, taking hold of Martha's arm so she wouldn't say their last name. "We'll look forward to seeing you."

"Goodbye," Cecil called after them. "And be careful. The storm, it be a bad one."

"We'll be fine," Jake yelled back, then took Martha's hand and hurried her down the path toward their jeep.

Nine

The rain began as Martha and Jake hurried down the hillside, but they were shielded from the worst by the dense canopy of foliage that surrounded them. Nevertheless the trees began to bend under the increasing winds, and the leaves shivered. Without the friendly glow of the sun, the green vegetation looked even darker and the very air seemed menacing.

"Maybe we should stay here till the storm passes," Martha yelled, her voice almost carried away by a sudden burst of wind.

Jake shook his head, putting his hat on her. "No, this will blow all night, I'm afraid. We're better off trying to make it back to the hotel now, while it's just starting."

"Good grief, if this is just the beginning, what will the rest be like?"

"Bad, I'm afraid. Sidney Howell was right about that, at least."

Another gust of wind took Jake's hat and blew it off Martha's head. When she turned to retrieve it, Jake stopped her. "Leave it," he called out over the roar of the wind. "It's not worth spending time on. Let's get out of here."

He took her hand and they dashed for the jeep. They no sooner emerged from the jungle than they were bombarded by pouring rain that drove into them like needles by the force of the fifty-mile-an-hour winds. Martha's clothes were soaked in mere seconds. Her blouse was plastered against her and her jeans became heavy with water. She clung to Jake as they struggled to the jeep, bent into the blast, their heads lowered to ward off the stinging spray of rain.

"How will you see to drive?" Martha shouted. "It's horrible!"

"I'll have to chance it," Jake yelled back, hurrying her into the jeep.

They found it soaked, with rain dancing off the vinyl seats and puddles on the floorboards. Jake inserted the key in the ignition and pumped the accelerator. The engine came alive with a cough. It spluttered, almost died, then caught hold and revved into action.

"Hold on, honey," Jake shouted, grinning at Martha, whose pale hair was plastered to her head and shoulders. She smiled back and gave him the thumbs-up sign. He grabbed her and kissed her soundly, then shoved the jeep into first gear and jammed the accelerator to the floor.

The tires whirred uselessly for a second as the jeep slid in the mud, then they found traction and took off with a jerk. The wind whipped the rain into their faces even harder as they turned the jeep around and headed for the Paradise Hotel.

Jake wiped the rain from his eyes and squinted into the driving torrent. Palm fronds whipped across the road as the trees were bent almost to the ground by the powerful wind. It whistled furiously in their ears, propelling the rain even harder into the jeep.

Even in the best of weather, the road had been bad. Now it was almost impassable. The ruts had filled with water and the rain had turned the dirt surface into a sea of reddish-brown mud. The jeep crept doggedly on, guided by Jake's steady hands, but the couple soon realized they were driving on borrowed time. Soon the road would become completely unnavigable and they would be trapped.

"Keep your eye out for a building or someplace where we can take shelter," Jake shouted to Martha. "We're not going to be able to keep going much longer before we get stuck."

Martha held the backpack over her head to shelter herself from the downpour. She squinted at the jungle, where the trees and shrubs were being torn asunder by the howling winds. Here and there a branch cracked under the pressure and fell to the ground, crushing the matted foliage beneath it. As they bumped around a curve, Martha thought she saw a flash of red on the hillside.

"Up there," she yelled. "I think I see a rooftop."

She'd no sooner shouted than Jake swerved. The jeep slithered in the mud and he called out, "Hold on!" The jeep continued to swerve crazily, then they were both shouting as it took a nosedive and headed straight into a gully at the side of the road.

The jeep bumped and jostled and careened over leafy debris deposited by the storm, then abruptly came to a jarring halt when the front wheels hit a tree trunk.

Jake kept one hand on the steering wheel and reached for Martha with the other. "Are you all right?" he yelled when they'd come to a stop halfway down the shallow embankment.

Martha nodded, her heartbeat hammering. She couldn't speak, could only cling to Jake's arm and shiver in reaction to the near miss. If he hadn't been able to control the jeep, they both might have been killed. As it was, Jake was cut on the forehead where his head had hit the windowframe.

"You're hurt!" Martha cried, and tore at her blouse for fabric to serve as a bandage.

"I'm fine," he shouted. "Head wounds always bleed a lot, but there's no damage done. Save your blouse, sweetie. We might need it more later on."

"What are we going to do?"

"Make for that house you saw."

He slid the backpack over his shoulders, then took her hand. "Come on, Mrs. Molloy, we've got more hiking to do. Where'd you say you saw the roof?"

Martha turned to get her bearings. They'd been coming around the curve when she'd spied the rooftop. She squinted into the jungle, trying to see through the driving rain and dense foliage.

Among the trees, she spied a spot of color and called out, "There! See? Up there! I see what looks like a red roof. Do you think they'll let us in?"

Jake grinned. "They better. We're not staying out in this if we can help it."

It seemed easier walking up the hillside because they went with the wind now, not against it, and suddenly everything seemed brighter. They were halfway up when Jake let out a yell.

"There it is!" He pointed to a small white stucco hut that indeed had a red-tiled roof. "Thank the good Lord for your eyesight, Martha. There it is."

"It doesn't look like anyone's home, though," she shouted in return. "I can't seen any lights on."

"They probably don't have electricity here. The most we can expect is candles, I'm afraid."

"Candles?" she repeated, smiling up at him. "Why, that's kind of romantic, isn't it?"

He put his arm around her and hugged her, then hustled her up the hillside. But when they reached the shelter of the front porch, they found the door locked and no one home.

"Dammit!" Jake muttered, peering in the window.

"What'll we do?" Martha asked, hands to her eyes as she, too, peered in the window. There seemed to be only one room. There was a small cot, a table with two chairs, and a fireplace with dry wood stacked near it.

"Well, we ain't going back to the jeep, that's for sure." Jake stood back and looked up at the roof, then tried the front door again. "We're going in."

"How?"

"Simple," he said, grinning. "Break the door down."

It proved to be even simpler than that. Jake put his muscular shoulder to the door and heaved his weight against it. It shuddered but held. Standing back, Jake heaved himself against the door a second time and it gave way beneath his weight, flying open and taking him with it.

"Are you okay?" Martha asked, hurrying in after him.

"Just fine," he replied, dusting himself off and examining the door. "It wasn't even locked," he explained. "It was just stuck."

They looked around and realized that the hut had been vacant for quite some time; but there were blankets piled on the cot and the stack of dry wood looked awfully appealing.

"I think we're in luck," Martha remarked. "We'll have a place to sleep tonight and food from the hotel."

"And there's a fireplace," Jake added. "I'll get it started and we'll be dry and cozy in just a few minutes." He looked Martha up and down. "Well, maybe it'll take you a little longer to dry off...." A slow grin appeared on his face. "My Lord, woman, how'd you get that soaked?"

"Speak for yourself, buster. There's no mirror here but I can assure you, you look as wet as I do."

"Here," Jake said, handing Martha a blanket. "While I'm starting the fire, take off those wet clothes and dry yourself off. No sense in getting pneumonia."

Martha stood and watched as Jake busied himself with the fire. It was enormously comforting, she realized, to have someone care about her welfare. She valued her independence, but she saw that it came with a price. Sharing one's life with someone, on the other hand, had numerous benefits, and she was learning about them firsthand.

She suddenly was filled with an incredible surge of warmth. It seemed to consist of equal parts of affection and concern for Jake, along with an incredible realization that she also had needs—needs too long neglected. She had assumed herself to be gawky and unattractive and had therefore slammed the door on a number of possibilities in her life, among them a relationship with a man. Now she saw that all sorts of prospects were opening up, not the least of which was a real relationship with Jake.

With that realization came a sudden desire to go to Jake and put her head against his shoulder, to take warmth from him—not from some silly old blanket. The human touch, she saw now, was infinitely preferable to that of possessions. Yet she stood uncertainly, hugging her blanket, unable to make the move so desperately desired.

"Hey," Jake said, turning to look at her, "aren't you going to take off those wet clothes?"

She simply stood and looked at him, hugging the fabric when she knew it wasn't the blanket she wanted, but Jake. But how could she tell him? A terrible sadness welled up in her. She couldn't do it; she couldn't take the chance. She was a coward, only half a woman, unable to reach out and pluck the only wonderful thing that had ever happened to her.

"Hey..." Jake spoke again, and this time his voice was softer, filled with incredible gentleness. He cocked his head and contemplated her, then rose from the floor where he'd been kneeling over the fire and came to her.

"This has been a busy afternoon," he continued, running a finger down her cheek, then gently brushing back her soaked hair. "You okay?"

She nodded, but still she couldn't speak. She could only look up at him, her eyes enormous in her face, filled with the sudden knowledge that she loved him. He'd brought her something she had never known before: a man's attention and affection, his warmth, solicitude and caring. For that she would love him forever. She wanted only to look up into his warm eyes, to drown in them, to let all her feelings loose in her own eyes, to silently let him know how much she cared.

Sudden tears sprang into her eyes as she realized she couldn't tell him. He would laugh at her—or even worse, feel sorry for her. This was only a temporary marriage; and while Jake might want to take advantage of the situation and enjoy himself now, when they returned to New York, he would want the marriage annulled.

"Good Lord, sweetie," Jake said, seeing her tears and taking her in his arms. "What's the matter? Are you frightened? We'll be all right, honey. I'm here. I won't let anything happen to you."

It was all too much. His solicitude, the endearments he used, the way he held her and protected her—they all merged and formed a huge lump in her throat. Inarticulately she let out a soft sob, then put her arms around him and clung to him, pressing her face into his wet shirt.

She held him so tightly she wondered if she were hurting him, yet she couldn't let go, couldn't leave the warmth of his arms, the safety and protection he offered. Yet it wasn't the storm that frightened her, it was life. It was taking a chance and offering herself to him, opening herself to the possibility of loss or rejection. She had lived too long in a protected world of her own making—one where she risked nothing, but gained nothing, either. Instinctively she knew that Jake was her lifeline, yet all she could do was cling to him. If she let go, she would lose him, and so she held on, stuck, incapable of acting even while she knew that her only salvation lay in action. She was caught, snared in a trap of her own design.

"Oh, Martha," Jake murmured, "I'm so sorry. I haven't been thinking about how this storm might affect you. Yet you seemed so brave when we were in it, so filled with light and laughter, that I guess I just thought—" He broke off, sounding frustrated that he couldn't express himself more clearly. "I guess I just didn't realize..."

And then she saw something that she never would have believed even five minutes before: Jake needed her, too, just as profoundly as she needed him. He, too, was inarticulate, unable to communicate his need, unable to plumb the depths of his own feelings and put them into words. They were two lost souls, struggling to find each other. Alone they were insufficient; together they were whole.

"Jake," she said, leaning back to look up into his face, "it isn't the storm that frightens me."

He stared down at her and slowly his face changed. He brought his hand up and gently smoothed her hair back, but this time his touch was filled with something new, something incredibly beautiful. He seemed to be seeing her anew, as if for the very first time, and what he saw kept him from speaking right away.

But his touch told her everything. He held her as if she were precious. A new sensitivity replaced his earlier teasing. Even his solicitude changed, becoming more profound, filled with a magical tenderness that swept through her on a shivering tide, bringing her even more courage. At last she knew she would take a step toward getting what she wanted. And even if the steps she took were small ones, they were at least in the right direction.

"Oh, Jake," she whispered, putting her arms around his neck and hugging him fiercely, "I don't give a damn about the storm. I'm glad it came. I'm glad . . . I—we—" She faltered, unable to say what she so desperately felt.

"Hush," he replied, placing a finger against her lips. "You don't have to say it. Just say you want it."

"Oh, I do! I do!" she said, hugging him more tightly. "Oh, Jake I want it so much! I'm dying for it. I—"

She was lost in his kisses. They were as torrential as the storm that crashed around them; passionate and filled with heat, as fiery as the flames that licked the dry wood— crackling, hungry, burning hot and free.

"Oh! Jake!" She was on the floor and he knelt over her, unbuttoning her wet shirt, his hands almost shaking. His lips plundered her, taking her lips, bruising the soft skin of her throat, fastening on the swollen tips of her breasts, sucking them into his mouth, laving them with his tongue. He tore at her jeans as she tried to wiggle out of them.

She pulled open the buttons of his shirt, then struggled with his jeans until they were both naked at last, lost in each other's arms, rolling over and over, sinking into the ecstasy of bare flesh against bare flesh, of mouths and lips and tongues seeking, finding, arousing to heights that soared into the wind-lashed heavens.

He rolled over and brought her atop him. She settled onto him, arching her back as he fondled her breasts. She found his manhood and straddled it, then gasped in delight as he raised his hips and massaged her from beneath.

"Oh!" She gasped and flung herself against him. He rolled her over and was on top of her, his mouth searing as he kissed a hot trail from her neck to her abdomen. His hand found her, massaged, cajoled, caressed, bringing her to the brink of ecstasy, then bringing her back again, teasing her with the possibilities of pleasure, raising her desire to a fever pitch.

She dug her fingers into his back and groaned out loud, arching her spine so that her breasts were crushed against his chest, glorying in the feel of her body naked against his, loving the way he touched her everywhere, leaving no place sacred. His lips followed his hands and she could only gasp, writhing beneath him, hungering for his entry, begging him.

He licked and probed her with his tongue and she screamed in pleasure, arching herself beneath him, lifting her hips, begging him not to stop.

She clung to him. "Don't stop. Don't stop."

"I want you," he muttered, his voice low with passion. "God, how I want to be inside you."

"Yes." She could only whimper now, so filled with heat and need that she felt she would die if he didn't continue. "Oh, please, yes...."

He knelt above her and ran his strong hands up her naked body, imprinting her with his touch. She moaned and reached for his manhood, taking it in her hands and caressing it.

"Feels so good!" he gasped.

"More?" she whispered.

"Yes."

She lowered her head and caressed him, arousing him to peak desire. He pulled the blanket up and she lay back on it, opening herself to him. He entered, then hovered over her with his hands on either side of her head, staring down at her as he lay buried deep inside her. She shivered and gasped and pulled him down on top of her, putting her arms around him and lifting her hips as he pushed himself deeper within her.

He went so slowly, she thought she would die. Ecstasy filled her, mounting to frenzy. He began to quicken his pace, each time filling her with greater heat, pushing deep inside her, finding her soul and mating with it. She had made love only once before, but it hadn't prepared her for the beauty of lovemaking.

She hugged him fiercely, sobbing her delight as each time he pushed deeper, each time a little harder, quicker, bringing her closer and closer to the abyss. She clung to him, crying, sobbing, laughing, at loose in the fields of pleasure, lost in the dance of love.

And then it mounted so rapidly, she lost control. Gasping, she clung to him, letting him take her away, letting him do with her what she so desperately wanted. She closed her eyes and threw back her head as he buried himself in her, holding her breasts in his hands while his mouth plundered the soft skin of her neck.

She screamed. It was too beautiful. It was glorious. It was heaven, and yet she was still alive. The skies opened and sun flooded the world. Golden rays shimmered behind her closed lids, filling her with light. She sobbed brokenheartedly because it was over, but then she clung to Jake, holding him close as she slowly came back to earth.

"So that's why the French call it 'the little death,'" she mused when the spasms had stopped rocking her.

Jake smiled contentedly and brushed her hair back from her forehead, depositing gentle kisses on her face. "Mmm. And we can do it again, and again, and again."

"Oh, Jake." She sighed, rolling onto her side to face him. "How wonderful." She was drowsy with contentment, warmed by his lovemaking and the heat from the fire. "Will it be like that every time?"

He smiled. "If we're lucky. But probably not. That was incredible."

"Yes," she agreed, smiling as her fingers caressed his chest. "It was, wasn't it?"

One corner of his mouth turned up. "And you were incredible. To think all those years I had a little sex-kitten in my office and never even knew it."

She laughed in delight. "I never knew it, either."

"Really?"

She nodded, drowsing as she rested with her head on his outstretched arm. "Mmm. I never knew it could be like this. I thought it was only in sexy movies and books."

He smiled and rolled on his side, cupping a breast in his hand. "You're beautiful, Martha," he murmured, caressing her nipple between his thumb and forefinger. He smiled as it began to harden at his touch. Leaning down, he sucked it into his mouth and twirled his tongue over and around it.

Martha closed her eyes, an enchanted smile on her lips. "Oh, Jake..."

He lifted his head and looked at her. "Good?"

"Wonderful."

"More?"

"Oh, yes, please...."

He cupped both her breasts in his hands and molded them, rubbing them to arousal so that both nipples stood firm and pink beneath his palms. "Thank God for this storm," he remarked.

She opened her eyes and smiled at him. "Mmm. How long do you think I could've held out against you at the hotel?"

He grinned. "Not long."

"Oh, yeah?" She sat up and drew the blanket around her. "Don't let your ego get too big, Molloy. Maybe once is all I wanted."

"Uh-uh," he replied, his grin spreading. He put his hand beneath the blanket and touched her nipples. "Nope, that's not what these little beauties are telling me."

She lifted her chin and turned her back, feigning disdain. "Ha!"

He knelt behind her and put his arms around her. Slowly he peeled away the blanket, leaving her naked in his arms. Lowering his head, he began kissing the side of her neck while he cupped her breasts from behind, massaging them in wide circles, her nipples rigid in his palms.

"I don't think that's what you want, Mrs. Molloy," he whispered in her ear. She tilted her head to the right so he could suckle her earlobe.

"It isn't?" she asked breathlessly.

"No...." He slid his hands down to her waist and brought her back against him. She tried not to gasp, but couldn't stay silent. "You like this?" he murmured, moving his hands down to caress the sensitive skin at the tops of her thighs.

She nodded, unable to speak. The eroticism that was flowering inside her had closed up her throat.

"Hmm?" Jake prodded. "Do you like it, honey?" He massaged her womanhood with knowing fingers, finding the pearl that brought her so much pleasure and fingering it lightly, teasingly, arousing her to madness.

"Yes," she whispered.

"Yes?"

She moaned in rapture. "Oh, Jake, yes...." she murmured. Her voice was no more than a wisp in the air. He was doing things to her she'd never even dreamed of, opening doors that led to places she hadn't known existed. She went with him, placing her trust in him, knowing he was bringing her to heights that would change her forever. She went gladly. She loved him.

Ten

<hr>

While one storm raged outside the small hut, another raged within. All the passion and desire that had been leashed inside Martha for years were set loose by Jake. She gave herself to him repeatedly, discovering pleasures she had only imagined before, joys she had thought were forever forbidden to her.

But finally normalcy returned. Exhausted, they lay on the cot, which they'd pulled up to the fire, and were staring at the ceiling, dazed by the incredible lovemaking they had shared that day. Then Martha's stomach growled.

"Good grief," she exclaimed, sitting up. "I'm starving!"

Jake chuckled and ran his hand down her smooth back. "Well, I'm incapable just now, sweetheart. Give me a break and take a rest."

"I don't mean *that*."

"You mean there's another kind of starvation?"

"Yes. This kind—for food, Mr. Molloy." She took out the insulated cooler their meal was packed in and opened it. "Oh, no!" she cried out, staring at the contents.

"What is it? Something you don't like?"

"No. Look, it's..." She began to laugh. "Oh, Lord, Jake, it's *chicken*!"

He burst out laughing and pulled her into his arms. "I wonder if they sacrificed it especially for us?"

They roared with laughter, then lay trying to catch their breath.

"Oh, my," Martha said at last, wiping away tears. "I suppose we'll have to eat it. I'm too hungry to refuse anything, right now."

"Good," he replied, diving at her. "I want your body... now. Here. Gimme!" He kissed her repeatedly— loud, smacking kisses that a two-year-old might plant on his beloved teddy.

She tried to beat him off, hitting at him ineffectually because she was laughing so hard. "Stop it, you silly man," she gasped when she was able. "Stop it this instant!"

"Listen to her. You always wanted to give the orders, didn't you, Martha? And now you think you can get away with it. Well, you can't." He blew a raspberry on her stomach, sending her into convulsive laughter all over again.

At last her giggles died away, leaving her breathlessly happy. She glowed as she looked into his eyes. Reaching out, she touched his face. "I wish it could be this way forever," she murmured. "This has been the most wonderful day of my life."

He looked at her, and his face grew serious. Turning over on his back, he put an arm over his eyes.

"Did I say something wrong?" she questioned, feeling a pit open in her stomach.

He took her hand and clamped it to his chest. "No, of course not. I just can't say things like that too easily, that's all."

She stared at him, her fear lessening. "It's hard for me to know what you're thinking, Jake, if you don't tell me."

"I know. It's just not easy, that's all."

"Do you think it's easy for me?" she asked gently, smoothing her hand over his chest. She smiled at him, all the love she felt warming her eyes. "But you've been so patient with me these past couple of days, I guess I can be patient with you."

"Patient?"

"Yes, you kept your sense of humor when I made things so difficult for you at the hotel. I knew I was your wife, but it wasn't easy to be around you in the room, Jake. I felt awkward, yet you never scolded me, never complained. You just kept teasing me, but you seemed so understanding. You never *forced* me."

"What good would that have done?"

"No good at all," she agreed, smiling as she rested her head on his chest. "I would have just gotten worse."

He rubbed her back. "Mmm. Even at your worst, you're delightful."

She felt chills run over her skin at his words. "Am I?" she asked, sitting up.

"You are. And now, Mrs. Molloy, I think it's time we devoured that chicken. I'm starving, too."

They pulled blankets around them and sat on the cot facing the fire, enjoying the delicious fried chicken, chilled soup and tossed salad, along with the still-cold bottles of beer.

"You know, we haven't had any time to think about what we found out today," Jake said at last.

"Good grief, I forgot!"

Jake kissed her. "Yes, in the heat of these past few hours, so did I. But it's time to put our heads together, Martha. It seems we've found out who's behind this whole mess."

"Bert."

He nodded grimly. "Yes. I couldn't believe it when Cecil Bongo said it, but who else could he mean? He said 'the man in charge' showed him the architect's drawings." He frowned. "But what I don't understand is, what drawings did he use? Our hotel is only one-story high. It's designed to be hidden from the bay. It'll blend in even more than this little red-tiled hut does. Where did Cecil get this skyscraper idea?"

"Perhaps anything built on that spot would be like a skyscraper to him."

Jake shook his head. "No, I think he really believes the hotel that's going to be built there is a skyscraper. I just wonder how Bert switched the architect's plans."

"But what about Oliver Thumpwhistle?" Martha asked. "He's certainly got plenty of reason to resent Hilliard's building here."

"Yes, he does," Jake said thoughtfully. "But right now, I'm more interested in seeing those plans than anything else. If Cecil's right, and I have no reason to doubt he is, then I'll have to confront Bert."

"That doesn't sound like a pleasant task."

"No, it isn't. I don't trust many people, as you well know, but I was beginning to think I could trust Bert."

Martha slumped back on the cot. "Yes," she agreed, feeling the disappointment Jake must be experiencing. "That's rotten, Jake. Come here, let me make things better."

He turned and looked at her. She lay naked on the cot, her platinum hair a pale aura in the firelit room. "Do you know, I do believe you're the only thing right now that could take my mind off work."

"Then come here," she said softly, gazing up at him with eyes that glowed with expectation. She now knew what to expect, and already her heart was thumping madly....

The next morning, Jake and Martha stood surveying the damage done to their jeep. "I'll need someone to help get it out of the ditch,'' Jake said, rubbing his day-old growth of beard. He looked at Martha and grinned. "Looks like we're going to have to walk a ways, sweetheart."

Martha stood on tiptoe and kissed him lingeringly. "Why don't we just walk back up to that nice little cabin we shared last night?" she murmured throatily.

"My Lord, how the woman does go on," he teased, smiling as he moved his hands up and down her back. "Give her a taste of the old Molloy magic and she goes wild."

"Poo-poo," she retorted, tossing her head. "I could have been marooned up there with a gorilla and felt the same way."

Jake cocked his head and studied her. "Really? We'll have to see about that. Maybe I'll arrange to leave you here with only a monkey as company."

She tossed her head again and set off walking, calling back over her shoulder, "You coming, Mr. Molloy? Or are you going to sit on your duff and contemplate the beauties of nature?"

"I think I'll walk a few paces behind you and contemplate a certain beauty I've recently gotten to know."

She smiled to herself but refused to let him see that his comment pleased her. "Talk on, Jake," she replied airily. "We've had our little interlude in the tropics. From now on, you're cut off."

"We'll see about that tonight, Mrs. Molloy," he said, chuckling. "I'll bet all I've have to do is crook my little finger and you'll come flying, tearing your clothes off on the way."

Something about his easy confidence maddened her. She refused to be taken for granted. Turning, she put her hands on her hips. "What do you take me for? Some sex-starved spinster?"

"You sure seemed like one last night and this morning," he remarked, with a knowing look in his eyes. He seemed supremely confident, as if he could take her right here by the side of the road if he wanted to. That only served to increase Martha's resolve. She'd be damned if she would let him think she'd fall into his arms at the snap of his fingers.

"We were trapped in a storm. Maybe I just decided to take advantage of our circumstances, as you suggested we do on our first night here."

"I see," he stated flatly. "I thought I knew you. But I guess I didn't."

She stared at him, but his face was inscrutable. "What do you mean by that?"

"It doesn't matter," he answered coldly. "We'll be going home soon, and all this will be over."

Martha's heart fell. Then last night hadn't mattered in the least to Jake. He was determined to end their marriage as soon as they returned to New York. She felt a lump lodge in her throat, and tears threatened to well up in her eyes, but she resisted them. She wouldn't let Jake know she cared. He would only pity her, and she couldn't stand the thought of that. She had some pride, at least.

They trudged along the still-muddy road, not speaking, their silence growing more and more difficult to bridge by the moment. They'd gone over two miles when a truck rounded a curve in front of them and began honking.

Sidney Howell was at the wheel, waving joyously. "Good Lord!" he called out, jumping from the truck and running to Martha. "Are you all right? We've been worried sick about you." He looked her over and smiled at her. "Yes," he said, his voice low so only she could hear, "you're none the worse for wear, are you, my dear?"

For no reason she could explain, she began to cry. "Oh, Sidney," she murmured through her tears. "Oh, I'm so glad you found us."

"Martha," he replied, his voice vibrating with concern. "Martha, my dear. You're quite all right now, I assure you. Quite safe, my dearest."

Without even knowing what she was doing, she went into his arms. She vaguely noted that he wasn't as strong as Jake, and being in his arms wasn't half as nice as being in Jake's, yet she stayed there, weeping like a silly fool into his shirt, when all along she wanted Jake to comfort her.

Sniffing, she peeked up to find Jake watching her, a sardonic look on his dark face.

"If it's all right with you, my *dearest*," he drawled, "I'd like to borrow Sidney for a few minutes. We might be able to drag the jeep out of the ditch with his truck."

Stepping out of Sidney's arms, she threw him a grateful look. "Of course, Jake," she said coolly. "Whatever you like."

"What I'd *like*," he growled to her under his breath, "is some time alone with you, but it will have to wait, unfortunately." He stepped away from her and turned to Sidney. "Would you mind driving back with me to get the jeep? It's in the ditch, I'm afraid."

"Of course." He turned to Martha. "Mrs. Molloy, why don't you get in? It'll only take a few minutes, I'm sure."

"No," she answered. "I'd really rather wait here."

"But—"

"Really, Sidney, I'll be just fine," she insisted, shooting an angry glance at Jake. He was leaning against Sidney's truck, his arms folded, watching them with that same sardonic look on his face. It would have been nice for her husband to be so solicitous, she thought wrathfully, but she supposed it wasn't to be.

"Well, if you say so..." Sidney said, looking from her to Jake uncertainly.

"My wife will be just fine, Sidney," Jake assured him. "She's a master of deception and cunning. Anyone trying to do her harm would have one hell of a time on his hands."

Martha looked at Jake, stricken by his words. Could he possibly mean that? That she was *deceitful*? But he was the one who'd proposed that she come on this silly trip and put on an act. She turned away, not wanting Jake to see the devastation his words had caused. But when he got into Sidney's truck without so much as a goodbye, she crumpled. Sitting by the side of the road, overlooking one of the most beautiful beaches in the world, she wept terrible tears.

What had happened to their easy camaraderie? Where were their jokes, their loving kisses, their hugs and laughter? Then she realized what had happened: Jake had gotten his way; he'd bedded her quite successfully, and she'd fallen into his arms, her eyes glowing, thinking everything would work out rosily.

Well, it hadn't, she had to face that now. Everything was the way it had been before they made love, only worse. She would have to spend the next few weeks with Jake, which would be excruciating; then she'd have the harder task of returning home and going through a quickie divorce while trying to laugh off family and friends' pitying comments and questions.

Then proud, practical Martha came to the fore. Well, she would simply do it. She'd hold her head up and refuse to let Jake see how hurt she was. And she would *never*, never in a million years, let him know she loved him. That would be the *coup de grace*—his already enormous ego would be stroked at her expense.

Intent on saving face, Martha dried her tears and resolved to carry on with dignity. It was all she could do; and she would do it well or die trying. Thus, when Sidney's truck appeared, followed by Jake's jeep, she lifted her head and stalked straight to Sidney.

"Can I ride with you, Sidney?" she asked briskly.

"Well, of course.... But your husband..."

"He'll survive an hour without me," she sniffed, and climbed into the truck, not even bothering to look at Jake.

What she hadn't bargained on was Jake. He was at the side of the truck in an instant, opening the door and pulling her out, none too gently. "Will you wait a moment,

Sidney?'' he asked graciously. ''My wife and I have something to discuss.''

''I don't want to discuss anything with you,'' she muttered under her breath as he guided her around the back of the truck to relative privacy.

''Well, you're going to have to,'' he said, his face grim. ''Just what the hell is going on?''

She lifted innocent shoulders. ''Whatever do you mean?''

He let out an exasperated sigh and ran a distracted hand through his hair. ''Look, we've almost finished with our business here. Couldn't you play along for a few more days? What will it look like if you start flirting with Sidney Howell?''

His words made her angrier than she'd thought possible. If she'd had any doubt about what came first in his life, she didn't now. ''Is that all you care about?'' she said in a low voice that trembled with emotion. ''Your stupid hotel and what people will *think*? Let me tell you something, Jake Molloy; I for one don't give a hoot what people think. And as for the Hilliard Hotel, I hope it goes straight to hell!''

With that, she turned on her heel and stalked back to the truck. Getting in, she threw a brilliant smile at Sidney Howell. ''All right, Sidney, we can leave now.''

But now that she'd taken her brave stand, her spirits slumped. She wished she could go back to the little hut with Jake. Everything had been wonderful there. They'd been blissfully happy. Maybe if she'd had a few more days there with him, he would have begun to really care about her. As it was, what did she have to look forward to? In a matter of days, Jake would resolve his problems on the island and they would leave. That didn't give her much time to get him to fall in love with her.

''Are you all right, Mrs. Molloy,'' Sidney asked after about ten minutes' silence.

''I'm fine,'' she replied listlessly.

Sidney frowned, glancing at her every few seconds, then looking in the rearview mirror at Jake's jeep. "Look," he blurted impulsively, "if he makes you that miserable, your marriage is no good. Divorce him. Things will turn out. You'll see."

"But he doesn't make me miserable!" she responded without thinking. "He makes me happy!"

"Well, pardon my saying this, Mrs. Molloy, but you don't seem very happy right now."

"Oh, you wouldn't understand," she said, feeling hopeless and helpless.

"Of course I understand. You married impulsively, probably because of physical attraction, and now you're realizing that you two have nothing in common. You don't share the same interests, you're vastly younger than him . . . Why, it's quite clear, Mrs. Molloy, you're just not suited to your husband."

Martha listened with trepidation. Was Sidney right? Was it just physical attraction she felt for Jake? After all, they'd worked together for five years without being attracted to each other. Maybe it was just proximity. Maybe she would have reacted this way to any man she was with.

While something inside her automatically rejected that idea, she still felt uneasy. Maybe Sidney was right. Maybe she couldn't trust her own judgment. Maybe this was her punishment for taking a chance and stepping beyond her emotional barricades. She fell silent, unsure of what she felt or who was right. She was lost in thought, trying to find her way out of this mess when Sidney pulled up in front of the Paradise.

"We're home at last," he announced, smiling at Martha. "And let me assure you, any time you need to talk, I'll be there for you."

"That's very kind of you, Sidney," she responded, forcing a smile. "I really appreciate your concern."

"It's more than concern, Martha," he continued, reaching for her hand. "I truly care about you."

"I...I see," she said, then frowned. "No, I don't, I'm afraid. I don't see how you could care about me when you've only known me two days."

"It happens," Sidney replied, staring at her with love-struck eyes. "Believe me, it can happen with a snap of the fingers."

Oddly, she did believe him, for that's precisely what had happened with her and Jake—or at least with her....

"Martha? Is that you, dear? What have you done to your hair? And how many times have I scolded you about not wearing your glasses?"

Martha wondered if she was hearing things. That sounded exactly like her mother. She laughed to herself. It couldn't be, of course. She turned her head in the direction the too-familiar voice had come from. Her heart jumped. It *was* her mother, hurrying toward the truck, waving a silly hankie while her father labored behind her, his solid bulk sweating in the afternoon sun.

"Darling!" her mother exclaimed when she arrived at the truck. "We were just too worried! We just got here. When they told us you were trapped in that horrible storm we were beside ourselves." Her mother's eyes went to Sidney and grew hard. "And this is your husband, I take it," she said flatly.

"Why, no. Actually, this is Mr. Howell, the hotel manager. Sidney, these are my parents, Mr. and Mrs. Simmons." Martha looked from her mother to her father, then shook her head to clear it. "But why are you here? I don't understand."

"We're here, Martha," her mother declared sternly, "to keep you from making a horrible mistake."

"What kind of mistake?"

"Oh, Martha," her mother persisted, shaking her head sorrowfully, "you'll never learn, will you? I'm just so thankful I spoke with that Miss...Miss..." Mrs. Simmons frowned. "I can't seem to remember her name, but you work with her. When I couldn't reach you at home, I called your office and she spoke with me. I couldn't believe you'd taken off just like that. I know you're deathly afraid of flying. Well, it was like pulling teeth, but I finally got her to tell me where you were."

"Laurie?"

"Yes! That's it." Mrs. Simmons shook her head disapprovingly. "A silly young thing, isn't she? Ah, well, comes from a poor family, I suppose. But that's neither here nor there. Your father and I came on the first plane we could catch. That dreadful storm held us up. No planes would fly out of San Juan, so we had to spend the night there last night, beside ourselves with worry." She looked around, her thin face filled with officious disapproval. "So, where is he?"

"Where is who?" Martha asked. She wanted to reach out and shake her mother, but then she'd always felt this way. Her parents never approved of anything she did, and consequently she'd never gotten along with them.

"Your husband, of course!" her mother snapped.

Before she could speak, Sidney Howell reached over and took her hand. "I'm sorry, Mrs. Simmons, but I can see you're upsetting Martha, and she'd had a very bad experience. She was trapped in the storm with her husband last night."

"Good Lord!" Myrna Simmons exclaimed. "You foolish girl! I knew we were right in coming after you."

Martha's spirits fell. It had always been like this. Her parents never worried about her; instead they scolded her. When she longed for their patience and understanding, she received the exact opposite. No wonder she hadn't wanted to tell them about her marriage to Jake. They'd have created a stink worthy of a hundred skunks.

"Mother," she insisted tiredly, "I am just fine. Nothing happened. Actually, something rather wonderful happened, but I won't go into that." She looked at Sidney, taking her hand from his. "Believe me, Sidney, I don't need you to take care of me."

"Well, you need someone to!"

Martha froze at the sound of Jake's angry voice.

"And who are *you*?" Mrs. Simmons demanded indignantly.

"I'm her husband," Jake snarled, opening the truck door and taking Martha by the hand.

"Good Lord!" Mrs. Simmons cried, waving her hankie under her nose as if she were going to faint. "Martha! How *could* you have married this crude, unshaven man?"

Martha looked from Jake to her mother and knew it was time to cut the umbilical cord for good. "I married him, Mother, because I love him. Now, if you'll excuse me, we have things to do."

She put her hand in Jake's and felt relief flood through her when he squeezed it and said under his breath, "That's the way, honey! Stand up to the old dragon."

"Wait!" Mrs. Simmons called after them. "You can't just leave like that!"

"She'll never give up," Martha groaned. "She'll follow us right up to our bedroom if she has to."

"Like hell she will," Jake blurted out. He turned to look back at Martha's mother. She was striding toward them, an implacable look on her face.

"Sir, I don't even know your name," Mrs. Simmons stated when she reached them. "But I know one thing—you have no right to take my daughter away!"

"I assure you, Mrs. Simmons," Jake insisted, "I have every right. Now, if you'll excuse us, we'd like to shower and go to bed." He smiled roguishly. "We didn't get much sleep last night, you see."

Her mother faltered, then lifted her chin. "The storm kept you both awake, I take it."

"No," Jake countered. "All the good sex did."

With that, he took Martha by the hand the they disappeared into the hotel, leaving Mrs. Simmons staring after them, openmouthed with shock.

Eleven

The minute they closed their bedroom door, Jake and Martha were in each other's arms. They kissed hungrily, then fell on the bed, tearing at each other's clothes until they were naked. They made love feverishly, as if this were the last time they'd ever see each other. There was no talk, no laughter—nothing but this incredible physical need, this frantic desire to join together and shut out the world.

When it was over, Martha lay with her head on Jake's chest, her heart thudding madly from their frenzied love-making.

"Did you mean it?" Jake asked.

"Did I mean what?"

"That something wonderful happened with me last night. That's what you told your mother."

"I meant it," she said softly. "It was wonderful, Jake. And this was wonderful. It's strange, isn't it? I just can't seem to get enough of you, yet we worked together for five years and I never felt any physical attraction to you." She rose up on one elbow and looked down at him. "Were you attracted to me at all?"

"Not physically," he replied, then frowned thoughtfully. "I guess I've always liked you, though. I can remember going to work some mornings and thinking about you. Sometimes I'd smile and wonder how you'd react to something, but I remember I always liked seeing you first thing in the morning. I always thought you were a plain Jane, but for some reason that was kind of endearing. I guess I thought you were a gem that I'd found and was keeping all to myself."

"I am a plain Jane," she stated wistfully.

"No," he said, running his hand through her hair, "you're not. You're incredibly pretty. You just needed a little makeup and some nice clothes to show yourself off. Now that I've met your parents, I can see why you'd feel the way you do about yourself. Have they ever once approved of anything you've done?"

She shook her head, lying on her back, staring up at the ceiling. "No way. My parents wanted a beautiful daughter, and they got me. I was the biggest disappointment of their lives, I think. They never stopped reminding me that I wasn't pretty enough. They'd always tell me to stop falling over my own feet, and that only made me more self-conscious. As I got older, I went into a kind of shell and I never came out."

"Oh, yes, you did." Jake said chuckling. "When you married me you came out of your shell with a vengeance." Then his laughter was replaced by a frown. "Our friend Sidney Howell is proof of that."

"Why, Jake Molloy!" Martha said delightedly. "You're jealous!"

"Oh, for crying out loud," he snorted. "Why should I be jealous?"

"That's what I'd like to know," she replied, eyeing him speculatively. Could he really care for her and not even know it? Or did he know he cared and for some reason wanted to hide his feelings? Or maybe it was just his male ego—he might not like the idea of another man coming on to a woman who was "his," even if she was his only for a few weeks.

"Look," he told her, sitting up and running a hand through his hair, "if you really like this Sidney Howell, then by all means, come back to him after we've divorced."

"I don't give a fig for Sidney Howell," she snapped, getting off the bed and heading for the shower. "And I wish you'd stop trying to plan my life for me!"

She turned on the shower and adjusted the setting, her temper simmering. Damn Jake Molloy. Why had he ever suggested that she marry him? It had led to all kinds of unforeseen complications, not the least of which was her falling in love with him and not wanting a divorce! But how could she tell Jake that? They'd made a business deal and she was stuck with it. If Jake was so blind that he couldn't see she was perfect for him, then she would let him have his silly divorce.

She climbed into the shower and soaped herself madly, taking out her frustrations on herself rather than Jake. She was covered with suds when the shower curtain was swept back and he climbed in beside her.

"What the heck are you doing?" she shrieked, her eyes closed against some soap that had gotten into them.

"Taking a shower."

"But I'm taking a shower!"

"Then we'll just have to take one together. Anything wrong with that?"

"Everything," she spluttered, trying to get the soap out of her eyes.

Jake put his arms around her from behind and drew her back against him. She went very still as he cupped her breasts and began massaging her nipples with his thumbs.

"Everything?" he asked softly.

She took a shaky breath. Never in her life had she done anything like this. The feel of Jake's hands sliding over her slippery body was as erotic as anything she'd ever contemplated.

"Well," she answered breathlessly, "perhaps not everything...."

"Good grief," Martha exclaimed when they were dressing. "My parents!"

"What about them?" Jake replied.

"My mother knows you're my boss. She could blow everything for us. Maybe she already has."

"Blast it," Jake muttered, frowning as he considered what might happen.

"What shall we do?" Martha asked.

"Track her down as soon as possible and find out if she's mentioned where we work. If she hasn't, try to talk some sense into her and ask her to keep quiet about it."

"Fat chance," Martha said. "My mother wouldn't recognize sense if it walked over and kicked her. Anyway, she wouldn't take too well to the truth, Jake. She'd faint if she knew I married you so we could come down here to spy on people."

"Then make up a story she'll accept."

"Like what?"

"Stick to the one you told her when you got out of the truck—that you married me because you loved me."

"But that wasn't—" Martha stopped herself before she could spill the truth—that it wasn't a story, because she really did love him.

"It wasn't what?" Jake prompted, his head cocked alertly as he watched her.

"It wasn't working," Martha answered lamely. "You saw how she reacted. The last time I told her I loved someone, she called his parents and broke us up in a matter of minutes."

"So, what's she going to do? Haul us into divorce court?"

"No, but she's likely to threaten abandonment. She'll probably say she and Daddy will write me out of their will."

"And she'd actually do that?" Jake asked unbelievingly.

Martha shrugged. "You can never tell with my mother. Sometimes she bluffs, but most of the time she'll do anything to get her way."

Jake studied her, then walked over and drew her into his embrace. "Growing up mustn't have been much fun for you."

"Fun?" Martha laughed without amusement. "No, I can't say it was any fun at all. I always...um..." She stumbled on her words because a sudden lump had formed in her throat. Hastily she wiped away a stray tear.

"You always what?" Jake probed.

"Oh, I don't know," Martha replied, drawing out of his arms and walking to the window. She put her hands in her slacks pockets and stared out at the lovely view. "I used to wish that I'd find out I was adopted. Every kid goes through that phase, I guess—especially when our parents fail us—but I did a little research and found out they really were my parents.

"Then I used to hope that someday Mother would see me and go through this amazing illumination. You know—that she'd see how unhappy I was and she'd just come to me and put her arms around me and comfort me instead of always telling me how stupid I was, or how ugly or awkward, or whatever she had to complain about on any given day."

She turned to Jake and looked at him curiously. "What are your parents like? I've never even heard you speak about them."

"A lot like yours, I'm afraid. I could never please them. They wanted me to go to college, and instead I dropped out of high school and became a carpenter's apprentice. They were livid. They disowned me. Luckily, Jim Hilliard thinks more of ability than he does of paper credentials, so my lack of formal schooling hasn't hurt me."

"Oh, Jake, I'm so sorry. Did you ever work things out with them?"

"No, I'm sorry to say, I didn't. They were killed in an automobile accident while I was still in my wild, rebellious stage. I've regretted it ever since that I never went home and made peace with them."

Martha went to Jake and put her hands on his arm. "I'm sorry," she said softly.

He looked at her thoughtfully. "You know, Martha, I've never spoken about it till now."

"How does it feel?"

He frowned as he considered his feelings. "It feels funny. I'm not used to thinking about it, much less talking about it." He put a hand to his chest. "In a way, it hurts. I guess that's why I've kept it inside all these years. When I heard they were killed, I went a little crazy. I punched a wall and kicked in a door. I wanted to destroy everything in sight, and I didn't even know why. And while I was doing all this, I was sobbing. It was horrible. I thought I was coming apart at the seams. When I got myself together, I vowed I'd never lose it again as long as I lived."

"And have you?"

"No, not even once. I developed this steely control over myself and pushed all that emotion into the back of my mind." He drew Martha into his arms and held her tightly. "God, it's good to talk about it finally, to know I *can* talk about it. I thought if I ever mentioned it, I'd fall apart again."

"You're not falling apart, Jake," Martha reassured him gently. "You're coming together."

"Yes," he said, moving his hands over her back and kissing the side of her neck. "Oh, Martha." he sighed. "Why are we dressed? I wish we were back at the little cabin, naked and in bed. I'd like to stay there with you forever."

"That's funny," she whispered, "that's just what I was wishing earlier this morning."

"Oh?" He stood back and looked at her closely. "So you want to run away from the world, too, eh?"

"No, I just want to be with you."

He stared into her eyes, then pushed her hair back with gentle hands. "When all this mess is over, honey, we're going to have to have a talk."

She felt hope blossom within her, quickly followed by a spasm of fear. Did that mean he wanted to stay married to her? Or did he still want a divorce?

"Yes, I suppose we'll have to talk about—things."

Jake studied her closely for a moment, then dropped his hands and returned to dressing. "But right now, we've got to do a little damage control. We'll have to find your parents and see what harm they've done. Then I'll need to find a way to see those hotel plans that Cecil Bongo spoke about."

"How will you do that?"

"Damned if I know," he replied, grinning at her. "But I guess something will come up."

They found Martha's parents in the cocktail lounge. Her mother was sipping a margarita and her father was drinking his usual martini. Both looked nervous and upset. For the first time, Martha felt compassion for them. Maybe they used the wrong tactics, but she supposed they really did care about her; otherwise they wouldn't have flown to the island to talk to her.

"Hello, Mother, Dad," she said, sitting down as Jake pulled out a chair for her. "Do you mind if we join you?"

"Not at all, daughter," her father responded. "But you realize you've upset your mother terribly."

Martha sighed. "I never meant to."

"But good gracious, child," her mother exclaimed, "you eloped and didn't even tell us! What were we to think? And to marry your *boss*—"

"Mother, that's what I need to talk to you about."

"Oh?"

"Yes, you see, um, Jake and I decided to get married and we wanted to be by ourselves for a while, because this was a rather . . . um . . . quick decision on our part—" Her mother groaned, but Martha ignored her and went on. "We decided to come to St. Matthew's, but we hoped no one would find out who we are. You see, Hilliard is building a hotel here and we were afraid we'd never have any peace if people found out that's who we work for." Martha peered at her mother. "You haven't spoken to anyone about who Jake is or where we work, have you?"

"Certainly not!" her mother said stoutly. "I wouldn't think of it!"

"Oh. Well, that's good," Martha replied uncertainly. "Why not?"

"Why not?" her mother echoed incredulously. "Martha, you've married beneath yourself!"

Dumbfounded, Martha could only sit and stare at her mother. What had happened in her life to make her so status conscious? The only things that had ever mattered in her mother's life were money and social position. Why did she persist in looking at life as if she were born in medieval England and were royalty?

"Myrna," Mr. Simmons interceded quietly, "you seem to forget—I, too, married beneath myself."

Mrs. Simmons went so white she looked as if she was about to faint. Martha merely looked from her father to her mother, so astounded she couldn't assimilate what had been said, "You *what*?" she finally blurted out.

"Martha," her father said, "it's time you learned a little family history."

"No, Edgar," Mrs. Simmons begged. "Please don't bring all that up—it's in the past. Let it stay that way."

"Myrna, it's been a shadow over our lives from the very beginning. I think it's time we explained what it's all about." Her father turned to Martha. "You see, Martha, your mother and I also eloped and faced terrible consequences from my parents. They said your mother wasn't good enough for me. And ever since then, Myrna's been trying to prove she is. She's gotten snootier than a princess, and twice as difficult to please."

"Edgar!"

"Oh, Myrna, it's true. I love you, but I hate to see what we've done to our own daughter."

"But Edgar, I've only done it for her own good! I haven't wanted her to go through what I went through—what *we* went through. Surely you understand that."

"Yes, I do. That's why I've never said anything till now. But Myrna, have you ever regretted marrying me?"

"Of course not!"

"Then who are we to step in and do to Martha what was done to us by my parents?"

"But—" Myrna Simmons stared at her husband, then closed her eyes and put her hand to her head. "Oh, Lord. I guess I've made a mess of things." She looked up at Martha. "Have I, dear?"

Caught in a bind, Martha couldn't speak. Her first impulse was to lash out at her, to unload all the pain and hurt she'd harbored for so long. But something held her back. All her life she'd been swallowing her anger, but now that she had a chance to unleash it, she realized the damage she could do. What should she do? Tell the truth and possibly hurt her mother? Or lie just to keep things comfortable?

She knew that neither recourse offered much opportunity for change. Anger unleashed might make her feel better in the short run, but it could lead to bad feelings that she might always regret. On the other hand, pushing her anger deep inside and pretending all was well would only make her anger grow. It would mushroom like a cloud, shadowing her life until one day she blew up, and then everything might be ruined.

She felt anxiety well up and wished she could take the easy way out. But if she made things easy now, she would just be putting off the inevitable. Taking a deep breath, she decided she would say something she'd never been able to say....

"Mother, all I want from you is your blessing. I need for you to let me be my own person, as Dad suggested. I need for you to let me live my life as I want to, not as you want me to. If that means stepping back and letting me make mistakes, so be it. At least they'll be *my* mistakes.

"All my life," she continued, "I've felt as if I always disappoint you. I didn't turn out pretty. I didn't do well at ballet—I was always stumbling over my own feet, as you used to tell me all the time. I didn't want to be a debutante. I didn't ever bowl over any eligible males. I feel like a complete failure as a daughter, but I don't want to be a failure. I just want you to love me."

"You ungrateful child," her mother returned coldly. "I do love you!"

Martha saw Jake's fist clench, so she reached for it under the table and held it hard. "Then show me you do," Martha said quietly.

"What do you want me to do?" Mrs. Simmons cried. "Good heavens, I've lived my entire life for you. I worried myself sick, hoping you'd find a man from a good family to take care of you, but you decided you wanted a college education. Then what did you do? You became a glorified *secretary*! I ask you! Is it any wonder I'm always upset? And here I come down here to find you've married this...this..." Mrs. Simmons shuddered and put her head in her hands. "Oh, dear, I've got a *splitting* headache!"

"Mother, Jake is a wonderful man, and I won't have you speaking about him like this. I understand you're disappointed, but you're disappointed for *yourself*, not for me. If you loved me, Mother, you'd be happy that I'm happy." Martha rose, clinging to Jake's strong hand. "I'm sorry, Mother, but I can't speak about this right now. I'm also getting upset. All I ask of you at this time is to not mention where Jake and I work. Will you do that for me, please?"

Her mother lifted her head. "I don't understand you. You're not acting like yourself. In fact, you don't even *look* like yourself!"

"Will you do that for me?" Martha persisted.

Her mother looked as if she wanted to walk away, but finally nodded. "Yes, we'll do that," she agreed, then lifted her indomitable chin. "In fact," she added coolly, "we'll leave tomorrow, so we won't be in your way at all. Will that please you?"

Martha felt herself wavering. She had a strong impulse to apologize, hoping things would return to normal, but something held her back. Perhaps it was the support she felt radiating from Jake. "If that's what you and Dad want, by all means do it. We'll call when we get home and discuss this further."

Astonished, Myrna Simmons stared at her daughter. "I don't understand what's happened to you!" she burst out. "You're not yourself at all." She looked from Martha to Jake and her eyes hardened. "It must be *his* influence."

"No, Mother, don't shift the blame to Jake. I've told you how I feel." Impulsively she leaned across the table and kissed her mother on the cheek. "Have a safe flight home, Mother," she said softly. "I'll call when I get home. Goodbye, Dad, and thank you."

"That was very brave," Jake remarked as they left the cocktail lounge and headed for the beach.

"I don't feel brave," Martha admitted. "I'm shaking, as a matter of fact. But I knew things had to change. All my life I've felt rotten about myself, but something's happened since I married you. I guess I'm beginning to see there is a chance for me, that I'm not the ugly duckling they let me think I was. I guess I finally got the courage to stand up to her, though it wasn't easy. Please don't call me brave, Jake." She turned and went into his arms. "Right now, I'd just like to be held."

"Someone once defined courage as doing what we have to do, despite the presence of fear. The foolhardy man feels no fear and rushes off to battle. The truly courageous person feels great fear, but does what she has to do anyway. So you *are* brave, my dear—whether you can admit it yet or not."

"Oh, Jake, when I'm with you I feel so good. I've never felt this way before. You help me believe in myself."

"Then even if the Hilliard on St. Matthew's Island falls in a flurry of chicken feathers, I'll feel I've accomplished something."

"Don't be funny, Jake. I'm serious."

"And so am I. You said something on that road today, standing behind Sidney Howell's truck, that made me think."

"Oh? What did I say?"

"I can't remember your exact words, but it was something about my caring only about the Hilliard. While I was driving behind you and Sidney, I realized that wasn't true, though it might have looked that way to you."

Martha looked into Jake's eyes. "What *is* true, then?"

"I care about something beyond Hilliard. I—" He looked away, startled by the approach of a man in a dark suit. Frustrated that they were interrupted, Martha turned to see who was approaching. It was the dark-skinned man they'd met on the plane, the one who knew about Hilliard's building a hotel on the island.

"Hello," the man said. "I hope I'm not disturbing you. Weren't we on the same plane coming over from San Juan the other day?"

"Why, yes," Jake responded, extending his hand. "I'm afraid we never introduced ourselves. This is my wife, Martha, and I'm Jake...Molloy."

The man didn't seem to recognize Jake's name. He smiled and shook hands, turning to smile at Martha. "And are you enjoying St. Matthew's, Mrs. Molloy?"

"Very much," she replied.

"Is this your first trip?"

"Yes," she answered, "it is. But you seem to know a lot about the island. Do you come here often?"

"Not often. But I've visited quite a bit lately on business."

"Oh? What is your business?"

He took time to light a cigarette, then exhaled and gazed toward the beach far below. "Yes, it's really a very beautiful island. I've been to many islands, but I've yet to find one as magnificent as St. Matthew's. It's as if the twentieth century doesn't even exist."

"But it won't be that way for long, evidently," Martha remarked.

"Why not?" the man asked sharply.

Martha shrugged. "Didn't you say Hilliard Hotels was building a hotel here? That would probably change the island quite a bit, wouldn't it?"

The man looked from Martha to Jake. "It might," he said carefully. "One can never tell with these things, can one?"

"I'm afraid we didn't catch your name," Jake interjected.

"I'm sorry, it's Wayne, Daniel Wayne."

"And you're here on business?"

"That's right."

"You neglected to tell us before, Mr. Wayne," Martha prompted. "Just what is your business?"

"I'm in leisure and recreation," he answered shortly. "But I'm afraid I have to be going. I'm meeting someone for a drink in just a few minutes. Very nice talking to you. Hope you continue to enjoy your stay."

He turned and walked toward the hotel. Jake and Martha watched him, then Jake said, "You did a terrific job pulling information out of him. You see? I'm doubly glad I brought you along."

"Doubly glad?"

"Why, yes," he responded, smiling. "Your company has proved very pleasurable on a personal level, of course, but you're also the asset I knew you'd be on a business level."

"And which do you like best?" she asked softly, going up on tiptoe to kiss his ear.

"Right now I'm enjoying the personal level immensely, but I'm afraid I can't split them apart. You're Martha, my faithful secretary and now my faithful wife. I like you both equally."

"Well, I'm afraid *I* can distinguish whether I like my boss or my husband better."

"Oh?"

"Yes. I like Jake Molloy, the husband, much better than Jake Molloy, the boss."

"And why is that?"

"Jake, the boss, never made love to me."

"So that's all you're interested in—sex."

"It occupies a great deal of my thoughts, but . . ." She frowned as she fell into step beside him. "Actually, I like you as a person, too. You're good to talk to. You're fun to be with—not just in bed, but out, as well." She sighed. "So I suppose you're right—I like both of you equally also."

"Good, because the boss is about to go into overdrive. We've got to find out what's going on at the hotel, Martha, before things get so bogged down that we can't get back on track.''

"So how do we go about that?"

"I'm going to speak with Bert tonight. Meanwhile, let's have a drink in the cocktail lounge. We might find good old Oliver and try to draw him out a bit about the island and the Hilliard building here."

"Do you think he could be behind Bert's plugging up the works?"

"He might be. He certainly has a reason not to want Hilliard to build here, and one of the first rules of our investigation is, find out who would benefit from Hilliard's not building. I'm afraid Oliver Thumpwhistle fits the bill very nicely."

Twelve

The cocktail lounge at the Paradise Hotel was a quiet, dark place, cooled by overhead fans and the tinkle of ice in glasses.

French doors opened onto a stone terrace, and lush green plants proliferated inside with almost as much abundance as they did outside.

Martha and Jake found a table in a private corner and ordered drinks, then looked around, hoping to see Oliver Thumpwhistle.

"There's Daniel Wayne," Martha commented, nodding to a small table in the darkest corner of the lounge. "I wonder who he's with."

Jake turned and looked, then immediately turned around. "Good Lord, he's with Parsons!"

"Parsons? You mean the real-estate agent who sold you the property?"

"Exactly." Jake put his credit card on the table for the waitress and took a quick swallow of his cold beer. "I've got to get out of here, sweetie. If Parsons sees me, we're goners."

"So what are you going to do? Get down on your hands and knees and *crawl* out?"

"No, my dear, I'm going to get up and nonchalantly walk out to the terrace. Then I'm going to rent that jeep and drive over to see Bert. Things are starting to go way too fast. I want to talk to Bert before anything blows up in our faces."

"But what about me? What shall I do?"

"Stay here and enjoy your drink. Stick around awhile and see if Oliver shows up and try to feel him out about things." Frowning, Jake glanced back at Parsons and Daniel Wayne. "Now, I wonder why Wayne is with Parsons . . . ?"

"He's in leisure and recreation—maybe he's looking for land also."

"Mmm," Jake said, stroking his chin thoughtfully. "I wonder." Jake's and Martha's eyes met. "Land to build a hotel, maybe?" he suggested.

She looked past him to Daniel Wayne, who was hunched over the table with Parsons. "Good grief," she remarked, "this place is crawling with possibilities, isn't it?"

"Fertile with them," Jake agreed, standing up and kissing her goodbye. "Wish me luck. If things go well, we might just have the answer to our puzzle by the time I get back tonight."

"Are you sure you'll be okay driving out there alone?"

"I'll be fine. See you soon."

He was gone before she realized it. She glanced at Daniel Wayne and Parsons and saw that they were deep in conversation. They hadn't even looked up when Jake left. She sipped her drink and thought about what they'd discovered so far: nothing much, but all of it was puzzling. She was still trying to make a coherent picture of everything when Oliver Thumpwhistle walked in and spied her.

"Ah! Martha!" he exclaimed delightedly. "I haven't seen you since your ordeal in the storm." He indicated the chair opposite her. "May I?"

"Of course," she replied, smiling warmly. "Please do."

Oliver settled heavily into the chair, then mopped his forehead. "Lord, it's warm. I think I'll order a lemonade. Join me?"

Martha shook her head. "No, I'm fine, thanks."

"Yes, well," he continued when the waitress had taken his order, "tell me about your adventure."

"There's not much to tell, Oliver. Jake and I rented a jeep to explore the island. We took a picnic lunch with us and ended up being caught in the storm. Luckily we found an abandoned cabin and holed up there for the night."

"Well, at least you were warm and safe. I met your parents, by the way. It appeared they weren't too happy with your unexpected marriage."

"No," she confirmed. "I'm afraid they're not." She couldn't resist adding, "But that's nothing new."

"So," Oliver remarked, smiling shrewdly, "you ran off and married the first man they'd disapprove of. Is that it?"

"No, I didn't marry him to spite my parents. I've known Jake five years, but when he proposed, I knew my parents wouldn't approve, so I decided to deal with them later." It was an abridged version of the truth, but it was true nonetheless.

"And I notice you sent them packing."

"Not true. They decided to leave when I refused to leave with them."

"And how do you feel about all this?"

"I guess I decided it was about time to start living the way I want to, whether they approve or not. I . . . I know I married Jake on short notice, but I do love him. If things don't work out—" She stopped because she couldn't go on. The mere thought of things not working out between her and Jake was now unthinkable.

"My dear, just hang in there and things *will* work out, I suspect," Oliver assured her. "I've watched you with Jake. I think you're both very much in love. You just have to learn to trust each other."

"I do trust Jake," she said, and realized she meant it.

Oliver smiled and sipped the lemonade the waitress had set before him. "Ah! Delicious! Now, tell me about your trip around the island yesterday. The place is magnificent, isn't it?"

Martha smiled to herself. Jake might have wanted her to draw Oliver out, but Oliver was doing a terrific job doing just that with her. She sighed and cupped her chin in a hand. "I love it here," she enthused. "It's truly beautiful. I've never been to an island before. I can't imagine any place being more wonderful."

"You're quite right, my dear. It's the star of the Caribbean, in my book. Harriet and I travel a great deal in the islands, but St. Matthew's is our favorite. St. John's in the Virgin Islands is quite similar, but even it can't quite measure up to St. Matthew's."

"Tell me a bit about its history. From the few natives I've met, it seems a fascinating mixture of old and new."

"St. Matthew's is like most of the Caribbean islands—it's a hodgepodge of cultures. Most of the blacks are descendants of slave shipped from Africa. But along the way they mixed in with South Americans and British, the French and Spanish, pirates and rumrunners. They came over to work the sugarcane that was grown in the 1700s and 1800s. Sugarcane is no longer harvested on St. Matthew's of course, but hints of the old culture remain. They are practically all Christians now, yet they persist in honoring the ancient island gods. It's a strange mixture, but it's oddly moving. They cherish this island and its ways. Though we've modernized with electricity and telephones and a small airport, they continue to seek guidance from the old gods."

"It's interesting you should mention that, because I've talked with a few of the natives—Jimmy, our driver, spoke of the gods, and our waiter and maid did, also." Martha drew patterns on the table with her straw. "And just yesterday, while picknicking, Jake and I met up with quite a character. He knows you, as a matter of fact."

"Goodness, they all know me!" Oliver said, chuckling. "Did you get his name?"

"Yes," Martha answered slowly, wondering if she was wise to open up this particular can of worms. "It's Cecil Bongo."

"Cecil!" Oliver chortled, his face glowing red with happiness. "My goodness! How is he?"

"Actually, when Jake and I met him, he wasn't too happy. We were about to settle down for a picnic and he chased us off."

"Chased you off?" Oliver frowned. "That's not like Cecil!"

"He was very friendly about it, of course, but he kept telling us that the gods would be angry if we had our picnic there." She frowned as if confused. "He said something about white men who wanted to build a castle here—a skyscraper is what he meant, we presume—and how he and his friends were guarding the spot so they wouldn't."

Oliver's red face grew serious. "And what was this spot like?"

Martha shrugged. "Like all the other places on the island—remote but beautiful. There was a magnificent waterfall nearby and the hilltop was shrouded with fog. It seemed . . . well, it seemed rather ethereal, as if we'd stumbled onto some enchanted place where we shouldn't be."

"Good Lord," Oliver said. "That's where Hilliard is trying to build their new hotel."

"Is it?" Martha asked, managing to sound ignorant of the fact.

"Yes...." Oliver was clearly troubled. He frowned at his lemonade, then lifted unhappy eyes to Martha. "You see, my dear, that spot is the holiest spot on the island. It's where the ancient island gods are said to live. Unfortunately it was private land, so no one had much of a say when the owner sold to Hilliard. I hear they paid a pretty price and he became rich overnight."

"Who was the owner?"

"Man by the name of Parsons. He dabbles in real estate, but hasn't madé much of a living until he struck oil with Hilliard. He used that money to buy up some other privately held parcels, and now we're all desperately worried that he'll sell to anyone who wants to build a hotel, thereby turning the island into a carnival."

"I see." Martha glanced at the table where Parsons had been sitting with Daniel Wayne. They were both gone, and the table sat empty except for two glasses frosted with condensation that dripped onto the tabletop.

"I wonder if you do see," Oliver commented. "This island is special, and we want to keep it that way. It's one of the few existing places on earth where one can come and find unpolluted waters and untouched scenery. We've made sure to take care of the environment here. We treasure it. The natives revere this island. They feel it's been given to them by God for safekeeping. It's a sacred place for them— not only their home, but the home of the ancient gods. The idea of this place becoming a tourist trap is abhorrent to them."

"But surely they recognize how dependent the economy is on tourism?"

"Yes, of course. We all do. But we also know there's a way to develop and there's a way not to. We're afraid Hilliard will come in and develop in a way that hurts the island, not help it."

"So the natives are using everything in their power to keep Hilliard from not building."

"What do you mean?"

"Well, Cecil said something about being a Mumbo Jumbo. That's some kind of holy man, isn't it?"

"Actually, it's a West African term for a magician who wards off evil spirits. As I said, there's quite a mixture here, so you'll find parts of African religion mixing in with West Indies traditions, including voodoo and obeah. But if Cecil were in the jungle by the waterfall, it's safe to say he feels he is doing what he must to protect the most sacred place of the gods."

"I've . . . heard the term *boo-koo*. At first I laughed, but is it real?"

"It's a form of voodoo native to St. Matthew's. Cecil practices it, I believe. It is not used to harm, though—only to protect. In most cultures, voodoo wards off evil through use of an image of the feared one. You've heard of people sticking pins in a doll and the person it's said to represent then dying of a heart attack." Martha nodded. "Well, I've seen it work. But here on St. Matthew's, *boo-koo* is used to protect the island and natives. It is a form of supplication to the gods, using images."

Martha shivered. "It sounds scary."

"To an outsider it can be. One has to really know these islanders to understand how peace-loving and good they are."

"But if they hold up construction of a hotel on a piece of privately held land, are they doing good?"

Oliver shrugged. "How do you define *good*, my dear? What's good for the Hilliard Hotel conglomeration might not be good for St. Matthew's. Have you ever thought of that?"

"I'm wondering how this affects you, Oliver?"

"Me?"

Martha wondered whether to play her trump card and decided to do it. "Cecil told us you own the Paradise."

Oliver looked genuinely startled. Reaching up, he mopped his forehead with his handkerchief. "I try to keep a low profile around here. It's disturbing that you found out."

"Why? Are you worried that people might think you have a vested interest in keeping out other hotels?"

Oliver's face grew beet red. "I have a vested interest in maintaining the beauty and tranquility of this island," he said vehemently. "It has nothing to do with commerce, my dear. It has to do with love. Can you comprehend that? Can you understand what this place means to me? We live in a world peopled by those who no longer care. They trample the environment, polluting our oceans and streams, destroying natural habitats and wildlife, plowing under precious trees and flowers and shrubs in the name of the almighty dollar or pound or franc. I will not have that here," Oliver declared, pounding the table softly. "Do you understand that, young woman? *I will not have it here!*"

Martha stared at Oliver, worried that his fierce outburst might bring on a heart attack. "Oliver, I'm sorry if I upset you. Please, calm down." People from other tables stared at him, then politely averted their eyes.

"Yes," he replied, mopping his brow again with a shaking hand. "Yes, I must. But you see, it means so much to me! I see this place as the last outpost, the last place left on earth where we haven't spoiled the environment." He sighed tiredly and drained the last of his lemonade, then held the glass up, signaling the waitress. "Another lemonade, dear, and this time add a touch of gin, will you?"

"Are you sure you're all right?" Martha asked worriedly.

"I'm fine," he answered, settling back in his chair. Suddenly he looked old and defeated. "I'm sorry, child, but at times I've felt as if I single-handedly have been holding back an insurmountable tide. It's coming, I know it is—the mighty surge of commercialism. Lord, how I hate it." He shook his head, then forced a smile for the waitress who deposited his lemonade and gin in front of him. "Thank you, my dear," he said. "This is just what the doctor ordered."

The waitress smiled widely and left, and Oliver looked at Martha. "I'm sorry to have made such a scene. Please forgive me."

"There's nothing to forgive, Oliver," she told him. "I'm sorry I got you so worked up."

"My dear, it's just that I love this island so very much, and I'm afraid it's all been a losing battle. Hilliard is one of those nameless chains. They don't give a dimpled damn about this island and its people. All they care about is money, I'm afraid. They sit in their boardrooms in New York or London and make decisions based on the bottom line—will they make money or lose it?" He sighed heavily. "It's plain to see, on an island as gorgeous as St. Matthew's, they'll make plenty."

Troubled, Martha saw in Oliver's face the despair of someone who had fought all his life to preserve something he loved, only to find he'd lost. She wanted to reassure him that Hilliard wouldn't destroy the island, but how could she? She needed to speak with Jake first.

"Oliver, what would happen if Hilliard built on another site?"

"What do you mean?"

"Well, let's say Hilliard found out that the spot they've selected is considered sacred by the islanders. Maybe they'd decide to buy another parcel of land instead."

"Ha!" Oliver retorted. "Such idealism! It's refreshing in a way, if it weren't so devastatingly naive. My dear, do you think Hilliard Hotels International gives a damn about what the natives feel?"

"They might."

"Oh, to be so young, so filled with faith!" Oliver remarked before taking a huge sip of his gin-spiked lemonade.

"Oliver, just for the sake of argument, play along with me. Let's say they *did* buy another parcel. How would the natives react? How would you react? Would you still be against their building here if they gave assurances to do so in an environmentally sound manner?"

"Ah, well, it's quite impossible, of course. But I suppose, given all those caveats, it would be all right. They're a good hotel chain. I've admired them for years. And if they really took an interest in this island and the people who live here, if they took the natives' wishes into consideration, then yes, I'd say it was fine. Contrary to popular opinion, competition doesn't hurt in the hotel business. The more people who come and see St. Matthew's, the larger the pool from which we can draw guests. We'll always remain a small, friendly hotel. We can't compete on the level of a Hilliard, and we don't try to. We offer a completely different ambience." He chuckled good-humoredly. "The Hilliard will never serve high tea in Spode china on sterling silver trays as we do. No, we'll always have a place on this island, even if the big hotels do arrive."

"Then I don't think you should give up just yet, Oliver," Martha urged. "You're a fighter. Keep your faith a little longer. Perhaps a miracle will occur."

"That's what I love about the young," Oliver commented wistfully. "You believe all is possible, just as I used to. It's only when one gets old and tired that things begin to seem impossible."

"Nothing is impossible, Oliver. Just remember that."

Oliver smiled. "I will, my dear, but I'm afraid you're much too idealistic. I used to be, but I'm beginning to feel as if all my ideals are archaic. Certainly very few people share them anymore."

"Ideals are what allow us to rise above ourselves, Oliver. If we didn't have ideals to believe in, we'd all sink into a sewer, thinking only of ourselves."

Tears misted Oliver's eyes. "This talk has done me an amazing lot of good," he said at last. "I begin to think that you may be right. And if you're not, I know damned well you should be!"

By the time Oliver and Martha left the lounge, most of the other patrons had left for the dining room. Having snacked on fresh fruit and a shrimp cocktail while having drinks with Oliver, Martha had no appetite for dinner, so she returned to her room.

Alone, she mused on how quickly she'd grown accustomed to Jake's company. At home, she lolled most nights away in solitary enjoyment of a good book or an occasional television program. Now she wondered how she'd done it for so many years. Her body yearned for Jake's touch; her lips hungered for his kisses. She wanted to put her arms around him and laugh with him and make love with him. She wanted to talk with him and sleep with him and share his meals—not just for the next few days, but forever.

But did Jake? Was he, too, growing to like sharing his life with someone? Or would be come all business, once he'd solved the puzzle of who was holding up construction of the hotel?

Unable to answer those questions and exhausted by the previous night and the day's emotional toll, Martha flopped on the bed and fell asleep immediately. She'd been sleeping for two hours when Jake returned. Though he entered the room quietly, Martha awoke anyway.

"I'm awake," she announced sleepily, sitting up and pushing her hair back from her face. "Did you talk with Bert?"

"Even better," Jake replied, sitting next to her on the bed, "I talked with Bert and Cecil Bongo, as well."

"Oh? Is that good news?"

"It's extraordinary news." Jake held up a rolled-up sheaf of papers. "These, my dear, are the blueprints that Cecil spoke about."

Martha's eyes lit up. "You mean it?" she said excitedly. "Well, show them to me! Did Bert confess? Did you fire him? What did he say when Cecil showed them to you?"

"Hold on, you're barking up all the wrong trees."

Martha sat back. "Oh?" She searched Jake's face. "Then tell me. What's it all about?"

"When I confronted Bert with the information, he flatly denied ever showing anyone any plans at all, much less plans of a skyscraper. Naturally, given my trusting nature, I didn't believe him for an instant, so he cursed me out and called Cecil into his office in the construction trailer."

"Good grief," Martha exclaimed. "So what happened?"

Jake shrugged. "Cecil agreed. He said Bert had never shown him the plans, the man in charge did. Well, by this time Bert was fit to be tied. He swore a blue streak and yelled that *he* was the man in charge. You know Cecil—he smiled and shook his head and said, 'Oh, no, Mr. Bert, you not man in charge. Man in charge told me you only supervisor of construction. He told me you take orders from him.'"

"Curiouser and curiouser," Martha remarked. "Are we through the looking glass yet?"

Jake grinned. "It grows better. Listen to this—Bert slams his fist onto the table and demands to know who this man in charge is, and Cecil says he goes by the name of Mr. Smith. Bert snorts his disgust and accuses Cecil of lying and Cecil gets very offended and promises not an inch of new work will be done."

"Good Lord, what a mess!"

"Exactly. So here's Bert ready to go head-to-head with the chief Mumbo Jumbo of St. Matthew's island, when

Cecil says he can prove he isn't lying because he has the plans.''

"No."

"Yes."

"What did Bert do?"

"He stares at Cecil and dares him to produce the so-called plans. That's when I know Bert wasn't involved with tying up construction. It was obvious he didn't know a thing about what was going on. Anyway, Cecil leaves and come back in a few minutes carrying these." Jake held up the rolled-up papers. "He unspreads them and what do you think we see?"

Martha shrugged. "The Mad Hatter?" Jake grinned and shook his head. "Ah," Martha said delightedly, "the Cheshire Cat!"

"Are you going to take this seriously or will you persist in making jokes?"

"Okay, okay, what was in the plans?" She looked at the rolled-up papers. "Actually, why don't you just show me."

Jake unrolled the drawings. Martha leaned over and studied them. "My Lord," she exclaimed, "they *are* plans for a skyscraper!"

"Precisely. And do you know which one?"

"No, do you?"

Jake nodded, pointing at a legend in the lower right-hand corner of the blueprints. "Castle Hotels, Ltd., Grand Bahamas," he read out loud. "I've seen it. When I went to the hotel convention last winter in the Bahamas, it was there in all its pink marbled glory."

"Is that why Cecil said the man in charge wanted to build a castle?"

Jake smiled. "I hadn't thought of that—perhaps it is, at that."

"But what in heaven's name does all this mean? Who's this Mr. Smith if it isn't Bert? You don't have anyone else working for you here, do you?"

"No, that's the final piece of the puzzle. If we can find out who showed Cecil these plans and told him he was the man in charge, and then figure out *why* he did it, we'll have solved the puzzle."

"But it doesn't make sense!" Martha said. "Who in Godfrey's name would trespass onto a hotel construction site pretending to be the man in charge, carrying bogus plans of some hotel that's already been built in the Bahamas?"

"How about someone from Castle Hotels, Ltd.?"

Martha digested Jake's words, then nodded slowly. "You mean they want to keep Hilliard from building here?"

"It's plausible, isn't it? What other reason is there?"

Martha nodded. "So all we have to do is find the man who gave Cecil the bogus plans and we'll have our culprits."

"It sounds that way." Jake cleared the blueprints off the bed. "But that can wait till tomorrow. Right now, I think there's something far more important that needs taking care of."

"What?" Martha asked. Good grief, was he going to do *more* work while he was here? "Jake, really, you've worked hard enough today, and what with that storm last night and all, we didn't get much sleep. Take some time off."

"I wasn't thinking about work," Jake responded, beginning to unbutton his shirt. "I was thinking more along the lines of pleasure."

Martha lifted her gaze from his chest to his face. "Oh," she said, beginning to smile. "Well, now you're talking!"

Laughing, they fell back on the mattress, lost in each other's arms.

Thirteen

I talked with Oliver Thumpwhistle yesterday," Martha announced over breakfast the next morning.

They were seated on the terrace at a small wrought-iron, glass-topped table on which lavender hibiscus floated in a cut-glass bowl. Plump strawberries garnished their freshly-squeezed orange juice, and kiwi slices furnished bright color to their plates of fluffy omelet and bacon.

"What did you find out?" Jake asked.

"A number of things," Martha said, studying Jake's features. In the past few days, she'd found out all kinds of wonderful things about him, but she realized they were enjoying a honeymoon in more ways than one. Right now, everything about Jake was wonderful; he was bathed in that halo of light that comes with the first blush of fulfillment of physical desire.

But what would he say when she told him the natives had good reasons for not wanting the Hilliard to build on the site Jake had selected? Would he be sympathetic to their plight?

Or would he snort in disgust and plow full force ahead without considering their viewpoint?

She was almost afraid to broach the subject for fear of what she might learn about Jake. After talking with Oliver yesterday, she sympathized with his and the islanders' desires to keep St. Matthew's as uncommercial as possible. But would Jake? He was a hardheaded businessman who'd climbed the corporate ladder one rung at a time, starting from the bottom as a carpenter some twenty years earlier. By his own admission, Jake lived and breathed the Hilliard Hotels chain. Would he put Hilliard's interests before anyone else's? And if he did, how would that affect her feelings about him? She could love a man who didn't share her most fundamental values, but would that love last? Wouldn't the wear and tear of their conflicting needs one day pull them apart?

Martha sighed to herself. She was jumping the gun, of course. She didn't even know if Jake wanted to stay married to her. Nothing had been said about their arranged marriage. It was possible he still wanted to return home and get an annulment—though they would probably have to go through divorce proceedings, now that they'd consummated the marriage.

At that thought, a black cloud seemed to hide the sun. Martha picked at her omelet, feeling sick inside. What a ninny she was turning out to be. For all her usual practicality and no-nonsense manner, she'd jumped headfirst into a real jam when she'd allowed herself to fall for Jake Molloy.

"Martha?"

Her head came up quickly when he interrupted her thoughts. "Yes?"

"Where've you been? I've been sitting here waiting to hear what you learned from Oliver Thumpwhistle, and you seem a million miles away."

"I found out some fairly important things from Oliver yesterday, Jake. I needed to digest them all—they may affect our business here on the island."

"I see. Will you share them with me, then?"

She smiled. Even at a time when he was obviously eager to hear her news, he was polite. That much she loved about Jake, even if he eventually disappointed her in other ways.

"Well, Oliver told me a great deal about the history of St. Matthew's and the natives, which explains why they're so reluctant to build a hotel on the site you've chosen."

"What *do* they have against building there?"

"Evidently it's considered the home of the ancient island gods. Though the natives are Christians now, for the most part, they still honor the ancient gods. The site you've chosen is the holiest spot on the island. In a way, what you've done is tantamount to some developer buying the land Lourdes is located on and deciding to build a hotel there."

Jake frowned as he rubbed his jaw. "I see. And Oliver sides with the natives, I presume." He laughed sardonically. "Does he also worship these native gods?"

"No," she answered coolly, "but he respects the natives' right to."

Jake grinned. "Looks like I stepped on someone's pretty toes. What else did you learn?"

"Did you know that Parsons owned the land you bought?"

"No. Are you saying he did?"

"That's what Oliver said. It seems that Parsons sold you that land, then proceeded to buy up lots of other privately held parcels on the island. Oliver and many others are worried that he'll continue to sell to developers who will then ruin the character of the island."

"So that's where Oliver come in—he wants to preserve the island as it is."

"And what's wrong with that?" Martha asked. "I think he's right to want to stop overdevelopment. St. Matthew's is magnificent as it is. Do you want to turn it into the next casino capital of the Caribbean, complete with neon lights, strip joints and nightclub singers?''

Jake sat back, a slight smile curving his mouth. He rubbed his jaw absently as he studied Martha. "My," he responded at last, "you're quite vehement on the subject. Oliver must have spoken quite eloquently."

"Jake, look at this place," she said, gesturing around them. "It's perfection. You can drive for miles and not see anything but the ocean, flowering shrubs and exotic birds."

"And an occasional goat or dog," Jake added, grinning.

She paused, two spots of red color appearing in her cheeks. "And those also," she agreed. "But look at this from a business viewpoint. Let's say you build the Hilliard where you want it. Construction will continue to be held up by the workers and you'll have earned their mistrust and anger. Who will want to work for you? How will you find maids and porters and kitchen help?

"And then, say Parsons sells more land to other hotel developers? Let's say this Castle Hotels chain buys land and puts up a hotel, and then all the others who've farmed the Caribbean tourist crop for years move in. Suddenly sleepy little St. Matthew's is going to turn into bustling Jamaica or St. Thomas or Puerto Rico. There'll be traffic jams at rush hour and horns honking at midnight. Is that what you want for St. Matthew's?''

"I'm afraid I don't have much of a say in what happens to St. Matthew's in the future."

"Of course you do!" Martha exclaimed, sitting forward eagerly. "All you have to do is buy up the land Parsons is selling and you'll have a monopoly on St. Matthew's! Then you can leave the area by the waterfall untouched and moved the hotel somewhere else on the island."

Jake's eyes twinkled as he drained his cup of freshly brewed coffee. "You have things all figured out, don't you?

Why even consult me? Why not just present your plan to Hilliard's board of directors and be done with it?''

"Jake, stop it. I'm serious.''

"All right, I won't tease you.'' He sighed and scratched his newly shaven face. "First of all, Martha, I chose the most beautiful spot on the island to build our hotel. I'd be a damned fool to give it up.''

"You'd be damned fool to build there, knowing what you know now!''

Jake ignored her heated comment and went on. "Second, who says Hilliard has a right to a monopoly on St. Matthew's? Who are you or I or Oliver Thumpwhistle or even the Hilliard board of directors to plan the future of St. Matthew's? This is a democratically run island. Are we going to step in by virtue of having lots of money and chart a course for the island over the next fifty years? Who's to say our ideas are the so-called right ones, or even the best ones? I agree that the islanders should have a say in their country's future, but if I did what you're suggesting, I'd take that say right out of their hands.''

Martha sat back, feeling deflated. "You have a point,'' she admitted reluctantly.

"I'm glad you'll grant that, because I grant you also have some good ideas.''

"You do?'' she said, sitting up again, excitement burgeoning in her face.

"Yes, I do. Your understanding of the locals' impact on our business is quite good and your arguments are lucid. I agree that building on sacred ground is hardly a propitious start to our project. Hilliard doesn't want to alienate the locals, and we don't want to harm the environment. Maybe we can work something out, but I see lots of problems. If we did decide to build somewhere else, we'd have to sink more money into buying more land. And frankly, I don't think there's a prettier spot on the island. And we still have to figure out who this Mr. Smith is, and why he's trying to drive us off our land. From what you've told me about Oliver, I wouldn't be surprised if he's behind the elusive Mr. Smith.''

"Oliver?" Martha questioned. "But he's such a sweetheart!''

"Maybe you're right," Jake conceded. "But Castle Hotels, Ltd. is an English corporation. Oliver is English, and according to Cecil Bongo, he owns lots of hotels in the Caribbean. I'm not saying Oliver doesn't have pure motives, but he may be behind our recent work slowdowns and stoppages."

"Oh, Jake, not Oliver!"

"Nevertheless, I'm going to call our legal department in New York and ask them to track down the owners of Castle Hotels, Ltd. If they're not covering up their ownership with lots of dummy corporations, we should know fairly soon who we're dealing with. Of course, it's entirely possible that Oliver isn't involved. But I feel more comfortable checking him out. That way, even if he isn't, we've eliminated one more suspect."

"And meanwhile what do we do?"

"I've asked Cecil Bongo to keep an eye open for this Mr. Smith. If he sees him again, Cecil will call me."

"But that might take weeks!"

"Do you have any objection to staying here with me for the time we allotted and continuing to enjoy ourselves?"

Martha smiled slowly. "Not when you put it that way," she replied, pushing back her chair. "So, what's our next step?"

"Well, the cat's almost out of the bag concerning our identities, so I think a visit with Stanley Parsons can't hurt. Want to come along?"

"Surely you don't think I'd let you go without me?"

Jake grinned. "I suspected you'd take that tack."

Stanley Parsons's real-estate office was located in a small white stucco building on the main street of one of St. Matthew's few towns, next to a store and a doctor's office. There was a wooden porch out front where a cluster of old men in shorts and T-shirts sat in wicker rocking chairs, peacefully smoking pipes. They smiled and nodded to Jake and Martha, then went back to rocking. The creak of their rocking chairs vied with the laughter of children playing and the barking of dogs. Otherwise the only sounds were the murmur of palm trees blowing in the breeze and water lapping against the jetties.

"Mr. Parsons?" Jake called when they entered the office. No one answered. Martha looked around, taking in the battered wooden desk and old swivel chair, the maps of the island hanging on the walls, and the few old magazines scattered on scarred bamboo tables.

"Looks just like a set for a forties movie starring Bogart," she whispered to Jake.

Grinning, Jake called out again. "Stanley?"

A teenage girl from the general store next door peeked around a doorway. "You want Mr. Parsons?"

"Yes. Is he in?" Jake asked.

"He with customer on other side of island."

"I see," Jake said. "Will he be back soon?"

The girl shrugged and smiled brightly. "One never know when he be back."

"What direction did he take?" Martha questioned, smiling at the young girl.

"Oh, he go that way," the girl replied, pointing west. "You can follow. He be in his car with the customer."

"Is the customer a man?" Martha asked.

"Yes, he tall with dark hair, wearing dark suit." She smiled again. "You find them if you go along that road."

"Thanks," Jake said.

He escorted Martha toward the jeep they'd rented. "You really have a way of getting information, you know that? I think you've stumbled onto your real calling—detective work."

"You mean you don't think I'm a good secretary?"

"You're a great secretary. Now stop fishing for compliments and tell me who this tall man with dark hair wearing a dark suit sounds like."

"I'd say Daniel Wayne."

"That's who I'm putting my money on," Jake agreed, grinning. "He's the only man besides Oliver and Sidney Howell I've seen in a suit since we hit St. Matthew's. By the way," Jake added as he drove off, "how *is* Sidney Howell?"

"I suppose he's fine, but since he doesn't give me daily bulletins on his health or whereabouts, I'm only guessing."

"Sarcastic, snide and the best damned answer I've heard in a long time."

"Why best?" Martha asked.

"Because it means you haven't had any further contact with the man." Jake slanted her a glance. "Or have you, and you're just holding out on me?"

"Why's it so important to you?"

Jake shrugged. "It's not important. I'm just asking."

"Ha! You're jealous, Jake Molloy, but you won't admit it!"

Jake glanced at Martha again, more leisurely this time. "Maybe I am, at that," he said. "You're looking very fetching today. I like that white blouse and pink flowered skirt."

"Thank you. It's part of the booty I picked up during my shopping spree, compliments of Hilliard Hotels International."

"Your boss must be a very generous man."

"*My* boss?" she repeated, laughing. "No way. He's a regular Scrooge. I can't count the times he kept me working late or asked me to come in on Saturdays. It got to be a girl couldn't have a personal life, the way that man worked me."

"Oh? Are you saying you'd like to have more of a personal life now?"

Her heart tripped over itself, then went back to beating normally. "That might not be a bad idea," she replied, keeping her answer as neutral as she could.

"And what would you do with it?" Jake asked.

She glanced at him and saw that he had his eyes on the road. His face was unreadable. She wished he would display some of his feelings once in a while, instead of interviewing her as if she were applying for a job. Then she realized that she'd passed one such interview successfully five years earlier; maybe she would pass another successfully now. If she just was herself, she'd be fine.

"I'd buy a house in the country," she said finally. "I hadn't realized how much I love flowers and shrubs until we came here. The thought of going back to my apartment in New York is depressing." She made a face. "I live in a building where the windows are all hermetically sealed. I breathe filtered air from morning to night. Being here, I've begun to realize how wonderful it is to breathe fresh air." She laughed. "Not that there's much fresh air in New York!"

"What's your apartment like?"

"It's boring," she replied. "I bought good, classic furniture when I got out of college, but it lacks zest. I think I'd like a home on Long Island, out in the potato fields. I'd fill it with books and flowers and plants, and I'd get a dog and a cat, and put sachets in my dresser drawers and potpourri in a kettle and simmer it on the stove and—" She laughed, her eyes glowing as she dreamed for the first time in her life of a future for herself, of days beyond tomorrow. "Oh, Jake, I want to live! All my life I've kept myself shackled to low shoes and neat little blouses. And you gave me the chance to break free and I have! It's wonderful, Jake—like learning to walk after you've been crippled all your life, or seeing for the first time, or hearing music when you've been deaf to all sound.''

Jake smiled as he listened, but when she glanced at him, she realized he seemed troubled. Startled, she wondered what he was thinking; whether she'd said something wrong.

''What about you, Jake?'' she asked. ''What do you want for yourself in the future?''

''Oh, I don't think I'll be changing too much,'' he said offhandedly. ''I'll stay at Hilliard probably till I retire. Just more of the same, I suppose.''

His words were like a knife in her heart. She turned her head to look at the brightly colored flowers that grew in abundance by the roadside, but tears misted her eyes, turning the landscape into a giant impressionistic palette. She'd hoped he would say he wanted to change his life by settling down with her, but those hopes were obviously dashed. Carefully she wiped away her tears so he wouldn't notice, then pasted on a bright smile. It wouldn't do to let Jake know it bothered her that he didn't want to stay married to her. When she returned home, she would have plenty of time for tears.

''But I might not have a future at Hilliard unless we find out who's behind this little scheme to keep the workers from building our hotel.'' He pointed up ahead. ''Unless I miss my guess, that looks like Parsons's old Chevy.'' He smiled at Martha. ''Come on, sweetheart, let's detect.''

Fourteen

Why, Molloy!'' Stanley Parsons called out. "What brings you to St. Matthew's? Want to build another hotel?''

"No," Jake answered. "I'd just like to build the one I bought property for."

Parsons cleared his throat. He was a tall, gangly man in a white suit and shirt, wearing a bow tie and a straw hat. His Adam's apple bobbed nervously in his skinny throat when he talked. "Yes, I heard there're some problems up there with the workers." He shook his head and sighed heavily. "Natives are like that around here, I'm afraid."

"Are they?" Jake said easily. "By the way, I'd like you to meet my wife. Martha, this is Stanley Parsons. Stanley, my wife, Martha."

"Nice to meet you, ma'am," Parsons replied, taking off his hat in a quick gesture of courtesy. He looked back at Jake. "So what brings you to St. Matthew's, then?"

"Work stoppages. Cost overruns. Complaints from my construction foreman that the workers have to sacrifice a chicken every morning before they'll do anything."

"It's their bloody religion," Parsons explained disgustedly. "They go to a decent Christian church on Sunday mornings, then worship those silly ancient gods the rest of the week." He shook his head. "What they need is a good dose of the twentieth century. Wake 'em up a bit. Make 'em see how stupid they are."

Martha stared at Parsons, aghast. "Is that why you're selling land as fast as you can to the highest bidder?" she snapped.

Parsons grinned slowly. "Hey, that's my business, ma'am. I'm a real-estate man. Got to make the bucks, you know."

"What about the future of St. Matthew's?" Martha questioned. "Doesn't that matter?"

"Ma'am, you may not like me—fact is, I can tell you don't—but that don't mean you or me or anyone else can tell what's best for this island. We depend on tourism for our living, most of us, and here we sit, the most beautiful island in the Caribbean for my money, and we're wasting it. We need to cash in on what we get, not let it sit idle."

"Like you did?" Martha asked coolly. "I hear you were wasting away yourself, until you sold that land to Jake for Hilliard."

Chuckling, Parsons took off his hat and scratched his head. "Yeah," he admitted, "that's true. I finally wised up. Why? That's what you Americans do all the time, isn't it? Make money. Spend it. Worship it, almost. I been readin' about your Wall Street investment types, making money like mad, and them yuppies, I think they're called, with their BMWs and frozen yogurt." He smiled and gazed around at the tropical paradise that surrounded them. "Yeah, I think what St. Matthew's needs is frozen yogurt stands, proliferating everywhere."

Martha stared at him and in a terrible instant, saw what the desire to progress, what commerce and civilization and the need to make a living were doing to the world, not just St. Matthew's. In a flash, she understood that when Jake set foot on St. Matthew's with the intention of finding land to build a new hotel, he'd set in motion a whole series of events over which neither he nor Hilliard nor Oliver Thumpwhistle had any control. Men like Stanley Parsons had been slumbering—hibernating perhaps—waiting for the catalyst that would release them to profit-making.

She turned and looked around, taking in the dense greens, the purples and lavenders, hot pinks and yellows, the low hills and sunny strands of perfect beaches, the air so clear it seemed to sparkle, the water so pure it reflected light all the way to the bottom. It was paradise, but how long would it last?

"Oh, God, Jake," she whispered, putting her hand in his. "What have we done?"

Jake squeezed her hand as if to reassure her. "Hold on, honey," he murmured, then turned back to Parsons. "Stanley, we heard you had a customer with you. Where is he?"

"Off wandering," Parsons replied. "Looking at land, just like you did a while back."

"For a hotel?"

"Yes, sir," Parsons confirmed, grinning. "Progress. The twentieth century is at last catching up with St. Matthew's."

"Tell you what," Jake suggested. "I'll make you an offer you can't refuse."

"Oh? What is it, then?" Parsons asked, wiping his forehead with his hands. "Hope it entails lots of money."

"More than you've ever seen or hope to," Jake answered.

"Fire away!" Parsons urged, chuckling.

"I'll buy all the land you own on this island. Name your price."

Martha suppressed a gasp, feeling her heart burst inside her like a giant flower shimmering in the tropical sun. "Jake!"

"Name my price?" Parsons repeated. "Golly, I don't know...."

"Only one stipulation," Jake added. "You have to name it now and agree on it. I don't want you waiting for this customer to come back to try to strike a deal with him and play us off against each other. Name your price now, and your land is sold and your money worries are over for the rest of your life. You'll be able to retire in splendor, sipping margaritas on a big terrace outside your palatial home."

"I can't give you a price right now." Parsons said, glancing up the hillside. His Adam's apple bobbed frantically.

"Fine," Jake said curtly. "It was nice speaking with you." he turned and walked away, practically dragging Martha with him.

They were almost to the car when Parsons came running after them. "Wait!" he yelled. "Wait a minute. Let's talk!"

Jake turned around slowly. "No talking, Stanley. Just name your price. How much do you want for every piece of land you own on this island—save the one piece where you'll build your dream house, of course."

Parsons gulped and stared at the ground, rubbing his jaw nervously. Then he looked up at Jake. He named a price that made Martha gulp. She stared at Jake, wondering what he would say. He didn't have the power to make these kinds of land acquisitions, did he? Not at *these* prices!

"Sold, Parsons," Jake said easily. "Draw up the papers. I'll sign them tomorrow."

Parsons burst into a radiant smile. "My gosh, my golly! I'm a rich man!"

"You are indeed," Jake admitted. "But I'm afraid you're going to have to disappoint your customer." He nodded toward Daniel Wayne, who was walking toward them.

Parsons turned around, then grinned. "No problem. First one makin' the offer gets the land. In this case it was you, Molloy."

"Ah, it's the Molloys," Daniel Wayne said when he reached them. "Out for a ride, are you?"

"Nope, out to buy property, just like you," Jake explained.

Wayne looked quickly from Jake to Parsons. "You haven't sold him anything, have you?"

"Sure have!" Parsons confirmed, grinning from ear to ear. "Every damned thing I own, as a matter of fact."

"Even *this*?" Wayne asked, pointing to the piece of land he'd just been surveying.

"Yup, every blessed inch of it," Parsons replied equably.

Wayne turned and fixed Jake with steely eyes. "Who are you?" he asked. "You're not just some guy here on his honeymoon."

"Oh, I'm here on my honeymoon, all right," Jake answered, smiling. "But I'm also clearing up a little business that needed taking care of."

"Such as buying up all the land on St. Matthew's?"

"You got it."

"But that's illegal!"

"No, I'm happy to say it's not. But talk to me in a week or so. We might be able to work out a deal. You can reach me at company headquarters in New York."

"You work for Hilliard!" Wayne exclaimed, staring at Jake. "Why didn't I guess till now?"

"You weren't expecting anyone from Hilliard. You were too busy trying to chase us off our construction site."

Wayne's eyes flickered away from Jake. "You can't prove that."

"Sure I can," Jake said affably. "All we have to do is stop by and see Cecil Bongo. He'll swear in any court of law that you're a certain 'Mr. Smith' who showed him plans to build a skyscraper and told him that's what the new Hilliard Hotel would look like."

Wayne slumped against the jeep. "Look, I'm only following orders from corporate headquarters. I just do what I'm told."

"The corporation being Castle Hotels?" Jake asked.

Wayne nodded tiredly. "They'll have my scalp for bungling this."

"Maybe not," Jake responded. "It depends on who's running Castle Hotels and why they wanted to stop construction so badly."

"You got me," Wayne admitted. "All I know is, my boss told me to scare off Hilliard and find the next best piece of land on the island and buy it." He nodded toward the property he'd been examining. "For my money, this is it."

"My money, too," Jake agreed. "Matter of fact, my money just did buy it. I'm afraid you're out of luck, Mr. Wayne."

"Out of a job, too, I wouldn't doubt," Wayne remarked. "You wouldn't need anyone at Hilliard, would you?"

"Wait and see what happens at Castle. If my guess is correct, you won't lose your job."

"Why not?"

"Because your mission's been accomplished, and you have this woman to thank for it." Jake took Martha by the arm and helped her into the jeep.

"Me?" Martha looked from Jake to Daniel Wayne. "What are you talking about, Jake?"

"Let's get back to the hotel and see if our legal department found that information yet. If I'm right—and I think I am—then things will become crystal clear very shortly."

* * *

When they arrived at the hotel, they found Oliver Thumpwhistle seated on the veranda talking with Cecil Bongo. Jake told Martha he had to call the company's legal department, and left her to talk with Cecil and Oliver.

"We're enjoying the sunshine," Oliver explained when Martha joined them. "You know Cecil, I believe."

"Yes, we met the other day," Martha replied. "How are you, Cecil?"

"I am happy," Cecil said, smiling. "But I am not sure you are. Underneath your smile, you look worried. Why must you worry on a day like this? Is not good."

Surprised at his perception, Martha nevertheless laughed off his words. "If I'm worried, Cecil, it's because I can't stand the thought of eventually returning to New York. It really is paradise here. I've come to love it very quickly."

"Most people do," Oliver remarked, smiling. "That's why we have so many guests who return year after year. They come here and forget their problems." He looked at Martha shrewdly. "That's why I'm wondering why you have anything to worry about. Did you bring problems with you, my dear? Is it your parents you're worried about."

She smiled. "No, Oliver. I know I'll be able to work things out with them." She glanced up when she saw Jake coming toward them. He carried the rolled-up blueprints Cecil had given him last night. Looking briefly at Oliver, he nodded at Martha. Her heart fell. She knew he was telling her that Oliver was head of Castle Hotels, Ltd. "But perhaps Jake can explain why I'm upset."

Oliver twisted in his seat and studied Jake's face. "I have the strangest feeling you two aren't here just for pleasure."

"That's right," Jake said. "We came on business, actually."

"Business?" Oliver echoed.

"That's right. The hotel business, to be exact. I'm vice president for hotel development at Hilliard Hotels International." He looked from Oliver to Cecil Bongo. "So in a way, Cecil, I'm your real boss, not this Mr. Smith who's been feeding you phony information."

"Phony?" Cecil repeated, his forehead wrinkling in confusion.

"That's right." Jake unrolled the blueprints and pointed to the words at the bottom. "See this? These are plans for Castle Hotels, Ltd. This is an actual hotel they built in the Grand Bahamas. But these are the real plans," Jake explained, pulling out another set of blueprints from his back pocket. "Take a look at them, Cecil. They'll show that our hotel is designed to complement its surroundings, not compromise them."

Cecil bent over the plans, then pushed them toward Oliver, who studied them carefully. At last he sat back and sighed. "It's quite beautiful," he said. "I couldn't have done a better job myself. My compliments, Molloy."

"Thank you." Jake rolled up the plans. "If you'd only talked with us, Oliver, you wouldn't have had to send Daniel Wayne to do your dirty work."

Oliver's face grew intensely red. He looked from Cecil to Martha and finally to Jake. "I beg your pardon?"

"You *are* head of Castle Hotels, aren't you? At least that's what my legal department tells me." He glanced down at a piece of paper he'd been holding and read from it. "Oliver Horace Thumpwhistle, chief executive officer and chairman of the board. Chief stockholder also. Founded the company in 1946 in London, right after retiring from the British Army as a colonel." He looked up from the papers he'd been reading. "Is our information correct?"

"Quite," answered Oliver, his shoulders slumping. "How long have you known?"

"Not long. I only confirmed my suspicions this morning."

"I had my reasons, you know," Oliver began to explain. "When I had Daniel Wayne sent here to delay construction on your hotel, I also gave instructions that he was to buy the nicest piece of property he could find. I was going to present Hilliard with a deal—give up your present site in return for the new piece of property. I figured Hilliard would only stand for construction delays for another month or two and they'd be ready to discuss my proposition." Oliver's shoulders sagged again. "I can see my plan went awry. You won't talk, will you?"

"Actually, we'll have a great deal of talking to do, but I wish you'd talked with us first, Oliver, instead of assuming we wouldn't listen."

Oliver snorted. "Would you? A huge international company like yours? I was young once. I, too, had visions of carpeting the Caribbean with splashy hotels. That's where the Castle on Grand Bahama came from, along with several other high-rise Castle hotels, on Jamaica, Bermuda, Antigua, Caraçao, Martinique..." He sighed and looked wistfully at their surroundings. "It wasn't until I grew older that I realized what I and others like me were doing. In the name of progress and making money, we were destroying a civilization and an environment. We were taking places like this and turning them into tourist traps. Progress," he pronounced disparagingly. "Is it progress? The older I get, the more confused I am about it all. I used to think we were opening this beauty for all people, that it was a beneficial thing we were doing. Now I wonder if I wasn't justifying my own greed."

He shook his head, looking old and very tired. "But in the past twenty years, I've made changes. I halted large construction on the smaller, less developed islands and focused on small hotels and inns, such as this one. When I found St. Matthew's, I realized it was the last of the undeveloped Caribbean islands. I bought this place and determined to keep it low-profile. I had thought I'd succeeded, until one day I found out that Hilliard had bought land here, as well."

He looked up at Jake. "Can you understand even a little? I love this island, and the people and their customs. To turn it into just another overpopulated tourist haven seemed a sacrilege. So I thought I'd at least try to scare you off the land you'd bought. That land is considered sacred by the islanders. To build there seems to me the most terrible thing we as developers could ever do. What right do we have to move into a country and use our money to alter the customs of the native people?" He frowned as he considered his own question. "You see, it's my own guilt speaking, Jake. For years I plundered and raped the Caribbean islands, and now I'm trying to make my peace with the islands and myself. I suppose I've done it at your expense, though." He sighed again and seemed to shrink in size. "Ah, well, it was a good fight. But time marches on, as they say, and waits for no man...."

Jake pulled up a chair and sat down, glancing at Martha, who watched Oliver with compassionate eyes. She looked at Jake and silently begged him to understand, to interceded, to somehow, in whatever way he could, accede to Oliver's wishes.

"Oliver, I don't think you've lost your fight," Jake said at last.

"Oh?" Oliver laughed sardonically. "I'd say I have."

"I just made a bargain with Parsons. Though Hilliard hasn't given approval yet, I'm going to ask them to okay buying all the land Parsons holds on the island. In return, Hilliard will give the site we'd chosen for our hotel to the government of St. Matthew's as a kind of national park, similar to what's been done on St. John in the American Virgin Islands."

Oliver came alive. "Why, that's simply marvelous! But will they do it? Hilliard is in business to make money, not lose it on good causes."

"If we can work out a tax abatement with the government, I think they'll do it. Say fifty years tax free on the hotel we build in return for the gift of five hundred acres or so to be used in perpetuity as a national park." Jake looked at Cecil, whose face was glowing with happiness. "That means your holy place will remain undisturbed, Cecil. No more sacrificing chickens to the gods every morning."

"Sacrificing chickens!" Cecil stared in confusion, then burst out laughing. "Is that what Mr. Bert tell you? That we sacrifice chickens?" Cecil chortled with glee. "Oh, no, Jake. All animals are sacred on the island. We no longer sacrifice them. I only carve the image of a chicken from wood. Every day we offer the image to the ancient gods in homage, pleading for them to halt construction and save their sacred home." He grinned happily. "And you see? Our boo-koo prayers worked! You stop construction!"

Martha felt a thrill of happiness go through her. Laughing, she shook Cecil's hand, and then, to her delight, she received Oliver's robust hug.

"As far as the land I've bought from Parsons is concerned," Jake continued, "we'll use a piece of land near the present site for our hotel, then hold the rest of it until proper zoning laws can be written. I'll suggest that all taxpayers on the island be invited to participate in the decision-making about zoning, new construction, the kinds of development the entire island wants. You're right, Oliver, and so is Parsons—development is inevitable, the economy of St. Matthew's depends on it. But it'll be up to the people of St. Matthew's to decide how they want the island to grow.

"Meanwhile, Hilliard will hold the land I've bought today until the new zoning laws and development plan are complete. By that time, we'll make a tidy profit selling land to other buyers. We won't hog the entire island to ourselves. We're willing to share, but only after we know that we'll have done everything possible to preserve and protect the peace and natural beauty of St. Matthew's."

"And you think Hilliard will buy your plan?" Martha asked Jake.

He shrugged. "We're in this to make money. I think if we can work out that tax abatement and then slowly sell off the land I've negotiated to buy today, we'll realize a tidy profit. It's long-term planning, but then that's part of my job."

Martha fairly flew out of her chair into Jake's arms. "Oh, Jake," she breathed, hugging him fiercely. "Oh, I love you, Jake Molloy! Thank you for listening, for caring. It means so much."

"Do you mean it?" Jake asked, searching her face as he smoothed his hand over her breeze-tousled hair.

"Of course, I mean it!" she replied, laughing. "I'm so happy. I think your plan is wonderful!"

"No," Jake said, "not about my plans for the island. Do you mean it about loving me?"

Oliver motioned to Cecil, and both stole away quietly, leaving Jake and Martha alone on the deserted veranda.

Martha stared at Jake, feeling her face grow pink. She hadn't realized she'd even said the words. They'd spilled out in a rush of gratitude, but she knew she meant them. Suddenly, protecting herself from hurt pride or possible humiliation seemed trivial. All that mattered was loving Jake.

"Yes, I mean it," she murmured, her eyes glowing with love. "I love you, Jake. I feel as if I must have loved you forever, but I never knew it until you asked me to marry you."

"Oh, God, Martha." He took her in his arms and squeezed tightly. "Lord, I love you, woman. And all along I've been afraid that once you got a taste of being attractive to men, you'd want your freedom. I've dreaded going back home, thinking I'll lose you to any man who whistles at you."

Tears glistened in Martha's eyes as she put a hand on his chest. "I'd never leave you, Jake. I want that home on Long Island, if that's what you want, too. I want flowers and sunshine and chintz slipcovers on all our furniture. But most of all, I want you—you and your babies. Little Jakes and

Marthas, giggling in the sunshine, all pudgy and pretty after their baths, waiting for Daddy to come home after work, to pick them up and swing them over his head and love them, and then turn to their mother and kiss her, too. Do you think we could have that, Jake?"

"I think that's the only thing I've ever wanted, but I didn't realize it, either. I always liked you, Martha, but I realized I loved you when I married you, when I saw you shining, glowing like a new flower who'd just discovered sunshine."

"You're my sunshine, Jake," she told him, resting her head against his strong chest. "I need you to be all I am. You complete me, you make me whole."

Jake nodded. "Me, too. I've been worried sick ever since the morning Sidney Howell came after us. You said something that made me think you wanted to dissolve our marriage, then you got in that truck and drove away with him and I thought I'd lost you."

"But I only said what I said because I thought *you* wanted to dissolve the marriage! I was afraid to let you know how much I cared. I thought you'd pity me. And I couldn't have stood that, Jake—not after what we'd shared in the cabin that night."

"Well, thank God for your mother, is all I can say."

"My *mother*?"

Jake grinned and put his arm around her, guiding her down the path that led to the beach. "Yes. When she showed up, your real feelings came out. You told her that something wonderful had happened during the night of the storm, and that's when I began to hope you really cared."

Martha began to laugh. "Can you believe it? Mother will have palpitations when she finds out she played a part in bringing us together."

"We'll have to deal with your parents when we go home, but I think when they realize how happy you are, they'll eventually come around. But right now, Mrs. Molloy, I have a yearning that needs to be satisfied...."

"Jake Molloy, you devil, what yearning is that?"

"Spending the next two weeks with you on a real honeymoon, swimming and snorkeling and making love on a moonlit beach at midnight. How does that sound?"

"It sounds so wonderful I can't even believe it yet."

"Begin believing, Martha. Begin realizing that all your dreams are going to come true. We're going to buy that house on Long Island and live in the sunshine, sweetie, just you and me and eventually the kids."

"Oh, Jake," she murmured, going up on tiptoe to kiss him. "I love you so much."

"And I love you—yesterday, today and tomorrow. Forever, Martha. Forever and always."

They wandered down the path that led to the beach— Jake's arm around Martha, her arm around him, two lovers ready to begin their life together.

* * * * *

Silhouette Desire

COMING NEXT MONTH

CANDLELIGHT FOR TWO
Annette Broadrick

Jessica Sheldon and Steve Donovan were related by marriage yet they shared nothing except mutual dislike. The man was gorgeous — but totally insufferable! The last thing Jessica needed was Steve's 'brotherly' escort around Australia; it was much too dangerous!

NOT EASY
Lass Small

Ruggedly appealing, determined, bossy, persistent — they all described Winslow Homer. He was a sweet-talking chauvinist who had never met anyone as infuriating as Penelope Rutherford. She was adept at avoiding predatory males, but there was something about Homer...

ECHOES FROM THE HEART
Kelly Jamison

Brenna McShane had never forgotten her very sexy — and unreliable — ex-husband. What was she going to do now that Luke McShane had returned, bringing home all the remembered pain ... and all the remembered passion of their young love?

Silhouette Desire

COMING NEXT MONTH

YANKEE LOVER
Beverly Barton

Laurel Drew was writing her ancestor's biography
when big, blond and brawny John Mason showed up
with a different story. Sparks soon began to fly
between this Southern belle and her Yankee lover.

BETWEEN FRIENDS
Candace Spencer

Catherine Parrish had waited a lifetime to hear
Logan Fletcher propose. But now that Logan had
asked her to marry him, he asked because Catherine
was his friend and not for romantic reasons. Why,
once they were married, did their old friendship
seem to elusive?

HOTSHOT
Kathleen Korbel

Devon Kane was the archetypal rolling stone. He'd
photographed world leaders, rebellions and
disasters, always hopping from one plane to another
and never making commitments. Then he was sent
to do a photo-story on Libby Matthews; what was
she hiding and did it affect them?

4 SILHOUETTE DESIRES AND 2 FREE GIFTS
- yours absolutely free!

The emotional lives of mature, career-minded heroines blend with believable situations, and prove that there is more to love than mere romance. Please accept a lavish FREE offer of 4 books, a cuddly teddy and a special MYSTERY GIFT... Then, if you choose, go on to enjoy 6 more exciting Silhouette Desires, each month, at just £1.40 each. Send the coupon below at once to: Silhouette Reader Service, FREEPOST, PO Box 236, Croydon, Surrey CR9 9EL.

YES Please rush me my 4 Free Silhouette Desires and 2 Free Gifts! Please also reserve me a Reader Service Subscription. If I decide to subscribe I can look forward to receiving 6 brand new Silhouette Desires each month for just £8.40. Post and packing is free, and there's a Free monthly newsletter. If I choose not to subscribe I shall write to you within 10 days - but I am free to keep the books and gifts. I can cancel or suspend my subscription at any time. I an over 18. Please write in BLOCK CAPITALS.

Mrs/Miss/Ms/Mr _____ EP99S

Address _____

_____

_____ Postcode _____
(Please don't forget to include your postcode)

Signature _____

The right is reserved to refuse an application and change the terms of this offer. Offer expires December 31st 1990. Readers in Southern Africa please write to P.O. Box 2125, Randburg, South Africa. Other Overseas and Eire, send for details. You may be mailed with other offers from Mills & Boon and other reputable companies as a result of this application. If you would prefer not to share in this opportunity, please tick box. ☐